The Portal Prophecies: Frost Bitten

**By
C. A. King**

**Cover Art By
Ryan M. King**

Book III in The Portal Prophecies Series

Copyright Page

This book is a work of fiction. Any historical references, real places. real events, or real persons names and/or persona are used fictitiously. All other events, places, names and happenings are from the author's imagination and any similarities, whatsoever, with events both past and present, or persons living or dead, are purely coincidental.
Copyright © 2014 by C .A. King

All rights reserved. This book or any portion thereof may not be reproduced or used in any manner whatsoever without the express written permission of the author and/or publisher except for the use of brief quotations in a book review or scholarly journal.

Cover Art by Ryan M. King

First Printing: 2015

ISBN 978-0-9940311-1-2

Kings Toe Publishing
kingstoepublishing@gmail.com
Burlington, Ontario. Canada

Dedication And Acknowledgement Page

This book is dedicated to my spiritual guide and psychic consultant over the past few years. Without her guidance and advice I may not have ever been willing to take a chance and branch out into something new and exciting.

~Suzanne Leocha Sadowski (ElegantOracles.com)~

and to the memory of James Huntington Turner who taught me anything is possible if you try.

Look for other Portal Prophecies Titles including:

Book I - A Keeper's Destiny
Book II - A Halloween's Curse
Book III – Frost Bitten

Coming Soon:

Book IV - Sleeping Sands
Book V – Deadly Perceptions

Chapter One

"We should tell her now! I can't stand the way in which the child lives."

"No not yet. She isn't ready. When the time is right we will. For now, she must wake and live the day as she always does and we must be there to help and protect her as we promised."

"But the prophecies, she will need time..."

"There are some things she must learn for herself. Too much too soon and she could be lost to us forever. Remember she is different from the others. Now pull yourself together and bid good morning."

*****

"It's time to get up sleepy head," a soft voice sang out gently in the dark. Willow opened her eyes and scanned the room slowly, instantly adjusting to the darkness. She never questioned how easy night vision was for her. It was a normal part of her daily routine.

Tilting her head from side to side, she looked over the room. There was a table, cupboards and a few storage chests. On top of the table was a bucket which collected water when it rained from a leak in the roof. Fixing it was on a list of '*one day to do chores*' that she hadn't quite got to. All the furniture was made out of the same aged wood as the building and needed the same amount of repair, including the bed she was lying on. She had one old blanket and a pillow, Martha the seamstress had made her. There were no lights or windows and only the one door. It was a place to sleep, definitely not a home. Scanning the room one more time she sighed. As always she was definitely alone.

"Come or you will be late and you know how the Council dislikes tardiness," a new voice, this one deeper, harsher, definitely a male, sounded loudly in her ear. She didn't bother to look around this time. She knew no one was there.

She had fantasized for as long as she could remember that these voices were those of her mother and father, but how could they be she had been told that her parents had died long ago. She had been only six cycles and couldn't remember what had happened to them. Nobody in town talked about how, just that they were gone, if they talked about it at all.

Willow sighed. Of course the voices were right. She had work to do and if she wasn't on time she would be in trouble again. The Council wanted things done a certain way, their way. As they had often said when she stepped out of line, "Our lives are like a puzzle. We all have to find the place where we fit in to make the bigger picture."

Her duty to the common good was assigned to her. She grew fruits and vegetables. That was her place in the puzzle and she needed to accept it, to do the very best she could. But still she couldn't help but feel there was something more, something she was missing, something she was destined for.

Her feet slid to the floor and she stood up, grabbed a pile of clothes from a cupboard and pulled them on. The female voice returned. *'Make sure you are completely covered. Remember what we discussed.'*

How could she forget? They reminded her every day. On her back there was a beautiful portrait of two stunning midnight black cats with crystal blue eyes and their kittens. They warned her to never show anyone the pictures on her skin and never tell anyone about their conversations, or the Council would be less than lenient with her. They never told her why, but deep inside she knew it had something to do with the past, something to do with what happened to her parents. History had been ruled a taboo subject and no one, not even the voices, would give her any information.

Willow opened a wooden chest and picked up a small hand mirror to look at herself. She hated the mirror. To her all it showed was her imperfections. Her eyes were a green and blue mix with speckles of red throughout. Everything else about her, she considered unremarkable. Her skin appeared as a lightly tanned, bronze tone colour, even though most of it never saw the sun and the places that did had freckles. She was above average in height and her work kept her in a physically fit state, which she felt made her some what less feminine than other girls.

Her long curly hair hung down around her shoulders. Today, it was blonde with a few blue and black strands. As with all girls, her hair colour would change on its own, as if it were matching her moods, abilities, or personality. She could have any number of combinations of hair colours in a day, in fact, last night she had gone to bed with pure white hair. This would continue until her sixteenth cycle, when her hair would choose the permanent colour it wanted to be. At one time, it had been believed the final colour of a girl's hair was directly influenced by the strength of her abilities, but the council had renounced that idea and they declared only council members and their families had the most powerful abilities. The women on the Council and in their families had many types of hair colours.

Like most of the under-aged, she didn't even know what her abilities were yet. When she was younger and out with her friends they would often sit and dream about different abilities and which ones they wanted. They had all been told the signs were there somewhere, subtle indications of the future and if they looked hard enough the answer was there. Once she had sat and concentrated for a full evening trying to make something, anything happen, but she ended up falling asleep out of boredom.

It was important to have the right abilities. It meant the difference between acceptance or a long, hard life of work and at times ridicule. If you could do something dazzling or entertaining, you might even get to stay on the castle grounds in accommodations which were far more comfortable than anything the town had to offer. Of course, on the other side some abilities were considered useless.

Her mind wandered to Victoria who was only in her tenth cycle and showing signs that she could heal bruises and cuts. Her parents had tried to hide it, but the rumours got out and the teasing began. One would think healing to be a good quality, but not in a world where there is no sickness or war, oddly enough she couldn't even remember the last time someone had died outside of what the council had declared. At least Victoria still had more cycles in which to develop other abilities. Willow was near the end of her fifteenth cycle and time was passing fast.

She looked one last time in the mirror, let out a frustrated groan and tied her hair back, which was already changing to a golden colour. Pulling the hood from her shirt up over her head, she said out loud, "Just get through the day." Turning to the door, she waited for the last of the rain drops to fall.

The rain fell at the same time every day. It started two hours before sunrise and the last drops dribbled down an hour later. Always the perfect amount of rain for the trees, plants, animals, drinking water, water to wash with and other daily uses. In fact the weather in general was always perfect, not too hot, not too cold, not too dry, not too wet and always the same.

Stepping outside she was greeted by a warm breeze. Closing her eyes she deeply inhaled the fresh air, enjoying every vibrant scent it carried, the forest, the plants, the gardens from the castle grounds and a touch of the smell of rain fading ever so slightly away. This is what made living worthwhile. She loved the fullness of the forest, with trees reaching high into the skylines and often climbed to the highest limbs of the tallest trees just to peak over the stone walls at the castle gardens with its beautiful flowers in all colours, sizes and shapes. Then there was the great hill overlooking the castle and the town. It was lush green covered with soft grass and four leaf clovers that could cushion a bare foot's every step, like walking on a cloud. Sadly no one was allowed to the top. The council had forbidden it, but it was beautiful to look at and it gave her world an unusual sense of calmness.

Walking around to the back of the small building she lived in, there was a large plot of land filled with vegetable plants and fruit trees in abundance. In a daily ritual, she gestured with her hands from side to side and thanked all the plants, trees and bushes for growing the finest produce. Her friends had expressed how unusual they thought she looked talking to vegetation but in Willow's mind that vegetation provided enough food daily for everyone and for that it deserved a thank you. She was pretty sure almost everyone already thought she was crazy anyways. Her mind wandered back to the voices and how quiet they were at the moment. Imagine what people would think if she told them about that. She let out a little chuckle.

"So don't tell them," echoed through her head. *"We have told you before not to tell anyone."*

Sometimes she forgot as much as she could hear them, they could hear her thoughts as well. She supposed it was much better that she didn't have to verbally communicate out loud with them and handle the glares and stares that talking to herself would bring. Deep down however, she was thankful for the voices. She had learnt over the years their advice was always sound and in her best interest. They basically had raised her since her parents had been gone and besides it was nice to not always be alone. Having someone to listen to her most serious problems made the hard times in life a little easier.

She placed empty baskets and bushels around the trees and plants and began to harvest produce for the market. After filling several bushels with tomatoes, squash and peas, enough to more than overload her wheel barrow, she pushed them round front to the market stands. When she returned round back all the rest of the baskets were full of peaches, cherries, apples, plums, grapes, berries of all kinds, carrots, potatoes, corn, beans, lettuce and more. She never questioned where the help came from but thanked whoever was responsible out loud and went about moving the rest of the baskets to the front.

The sun was just rising over the great hill and everything was still quiet. The town was made up of buildings that all looked the same on the outside, built out of ageing wood which was a greyish colour, with newer patches, made out of whatever wood was available where rot couldn't be ignored. Appearance wasn't a concern as long as any holes were covered as best as could be. There were no fancy designs, no gardens. These houses had been built strictly for need, the bigger the family, the bigger the house. Some people had added a couple steps or a porch out front perhaps to try to make for a more inviting sense of home or perhaps because some had a front room where they worked and showed people their products.

There was one main dirt and rock road that ran from the castle gates to the north, down through the town and ended at the orphanage. The forest bordered around the buildings to the south where it connected to the base of the great hill to the east. To the west the forest bordered the town all the way to the stone walls of the castle. No one had ever ventured to find where or if the forest ended.

Across from Willow's was Mrs. Waddington's place. She was the finest and only book writer and a talented story teller. Unfortunately, there was less and less need for books since the Council declared learning to read, actually learning at all, wasn't necessary. Still the under-aged would sneak out after dark whenever possible to listen to one of her wondrous tales of great beasts, love, deceit, war and peace. Her words could fly through the room and create visions of the very stories she was telling, as if it was happening before your eyes, and invoke the emotions of the characters she spoke of. There wasn't a lot of entertainment for children and young adults in the town, and story time was the favourite on everyone's list.

Beside Mrs. Waddington's place was the seamstress Martha who made everything from blankets to dresses and her husband Olie made shoes. Then was the Posh place for dishes and candles, at the end of the street was the Shinning house which made anything you needed out of gem stones, mainly jewelry for the Council. Across from them was the Miller bakery, which made the most wonderful fresh bread that melted in your mouth and danced on the taste buds.

There were other houses not on the main market street, with various different professions, woodworking, tool making and sharpening, metal working, mainly people who made the larger things you would order to be made for a specific need and various forms of crafters and animal farmers.

Willow finished setting up her market stands as the last of the night silently whisked away to make room for the light of day.

An hour later and the town was starting to show signs of life, although most of the store fronts wouldn't open for hours yet. People were moving about starting their chores and gathering water from old barrels for their daily needs. Jessie, Dezi and Pete, the gem worker's boys, sat on their front porch watching every last detail that was happening while their mother and father began to prepare for the day. Willow didn't envy them, knowing their only customers were council members and their families, who were always hard to please, each one wanting something bigger, brighter and more outstanding than the other. Across from the produce stand Mrs. Waddington was sweeping her porch. After her husband, son and daughter-in-law were all declared dead by the council, she had been left raising her grandson, Nathan alone. All of a sudden she motioned a fast waive and quickly moved inside.

A silence fell over the market place which could only mean one thing, the council was in town to pick up their fresh produce for the day. Council members enjoyed a fresh fruit breakfast every morning and were always served first before anyone else in town. Willow looked down the lane and held her breathe. Today wasn't starting off well at all. The council had sent their children into town this morning to fetch the castle needs. Rumours had been flying around town that council family members close to their sixteenth cycle were being given more duties to prepare them for the future. Unfortunately, it looked like they weren't just rumours anymore.

Malarchy and Nebulah's daughter, Jade was leading the teen group as usual. She was slim, with a white complexion, perfectly rosy cheeks and plump red lips. Her eyes were a deep green which flickered specks of emerald in the light matching her name and her hair hadn't changed in three cycles now from a light blonde colour. She always seemed to effortlessly control the style, which changed more often than her clothes. Today it was curly, not a natural curl, but more a manufactured one. Sometimes it was hard to tell if it was just the different hairstyles or if her facial features were different daily as well. It had been known for some time that appearance especially her hair, was one of her talents and she was quite proud to show off the glamour she could create. To complete her look today a frilly white dress hugged the curves of her body which were far more developed than any other girls her age. Following closely behind were Sabrina and Camile, who both tried to copy the same look as their leader, right down to the curls.

Willow winced as she imagined the two girls having to roll pine cones in their wet hair and then even worse remove them when their hair was dry. For the moment she was glad she had natural curls.

Behind them walked two boys, Justin and Neil, who weren't paying much attention to anything going on around them except for the rock they were kicking back and forth between them. Willow figured they were as good looking as boys get. Both were tall with sandy coloured hair and hazel eyes, medium build and dressed well. She didn't understand the other girls fuss over boys. They were okay, some were fun to hang out with and play games, but she hadn't ever felt gushy mushy gooey like the other girls her age did at the sight of any one or another.

Willow had been so distracted she hadn't noticed her best friend come over to sit beside her.

"Too bad she has to open her mouth," Clairity said referring to Jade.

"What would get you up so early?"

Clairity laughed and replied, "I couldn't leave you to deal with that lot alone now could I?"

Clairity was short, with an average build, not a stunning beauty, but she had style. Her hair was cut in an uneven bob which hugged her face in all the right places and highlighted her high cheek bones. Today her hair was black. Willow couldn't help but think that of all the colours the black definitely suited her the best, and it also matched her eyes which were such a dark brown you could easily mistake them for black. Her skin was a pale white, perfect like the porcelain dishes and figures her mother made. It made Willow laugh when Clairity's mother would pinch her cheeks as hard as she could to try to add a little colour to her daughter's face.

"Can we get some service here? Or do you think wasting our time is in your best interest?" snarled the girl in front of her.

Willow looked up directly into a pair of icy green eyes staring back at her. They were as cold as they were beautiful. She shivered as if a chilled wind had blown on bare skin, goosebumps forming on her arms, as she put together a basket of produce for Jade. Luckily, Clairity was there and had already started putting baskets together for the rest of the group. It was odd, but lately it seemed her friend knew exactly where and when she was needed or should be.

"Staring into space as we wait, pathetic. Wait till father finds out about this!" Jade said in a voice loud enough to be heard by most of the town. "And what is she wearing?" The three girls burst into a high pitched laughter together before heading down the road, not back the way they had come but further down the lane.

Willow knew the three girls were strolling toward the boys still sitting on their step. Sure enough they offered a flirting wave and a giggle. That was all it took to gain the boys attention and soon they were all talking and laughing together.

The two boys from the council group were oblivious to what the girls were doing, they were far too preoccupied with the delightful aroma of fresh baked bread coming from the stone oven out back of the bakery.

Clairity gave her a nudge. "Anyone home?" she asked.

Willow shook her head, breaking free from the trance she had been completely engulfed in. She looked up at her friend who motioned to basically the rest of town waiting in line for their baskets for the day. The two girls knew everyone in town and after the line had ceased they made up baskets for anyone who hadn't been by yet and together they delivered them. The last basket Clairity took home with her.

All that was left to do now was to pack all the remaining fruits and vegetables into boxes for the orphanage. The children living there had it the hardest. They had to share everything and they had very little to start with. Compared to the way these kids had to live, Willow was in a dream land. She felt sorry for them. Truly the only hope they had was to develop some ability the council might find entertaining or extremely useful. Willow made sure every day there was something especially yummy in the boxes, a sort of treat they could look forward to. After all, if circumstances had been a little bit different she might have been living there as well. She didn't know why she wasn't but figured the orphanage was already full by the time her parents had died.

She felt a tap on her shoulder. "Need some help with those?" Jessie asked. Usually one of the three boys would offer to help carry some of the boxes and Willow was glad for the help since it meant one trip instead of two, not to mention company along the way. As much as she wanted to help the orphanage she hated going there as well. It was dark, musty, and the last few times it left her with an uneasy feeling, like someone was listening and recording her every move while she was there.

Jessie was the tallest of the triplet brothers. Usually children born together look identical. Not in the case of these brothers. They were each different in appearance and personality. It was almost as if they were three parts to one whole person, each getting different qualities. The only thing they had in common at all was the light brown shade of their hair and matching eye colour. Jessie was muscular and very strong looking, but quiet. Dezi was just shorter than his brother and wasn't overly muscular but had defined shape to his arms and chest which suited him. He was loud, fun and exciting, the life of the party. The final brother Pete was the shortest of the three, although still taller than most boys their age and was quick to offer his opinion when he had one. He was neither boring nor remarkable, but could captivate an audience when he chose to. Most of the time, however, he was lost somewhere in the shadows of his brothers.

The orphanage was located on the far side of town and was the largest building other than the castle. The outside was weathered and old, definitely in need of major repairs. Inside were four rooms, the first was a small sitting room for visitors. Willow couldn't imagine that they had many visitors, but supposed it made Penelope and Micca feel better in case on the odd chance someone did drop in. Peaking in the door to the small room, it appeared as she had thought. The room didn't look as if it had been used in a very long time. There was a layer of dust on the furniture. In the centre of the room was a table with a tiny porcelain vase filled with what appeared to be dead wild flowers from the forest. The seats were benches with high backs and had some faded cushions that looked like they had been in the same spot since the beginning of time. Directly across the hall was the second room which was Penelope and Micca's bedroom.

There was an unsettling silence in the front areas of the house for having so many children. The hallway led to a tall wooden door, which opened into a food preparation room. The makeshift kitchen wasn't large and had cupboards that lined all of the walls. In the centre of the room was one wooden table, the sort you would stand at, not sit. Willow and Jessie lifted the boxes onto the table. Usually someone would have greeted them before now. Neither had been past that point before or seen the large room that the children spent the majority of their lives in. Out of concern and a little curiosity the two opened the door to the main room. The door itself was a heavier wood than the rest they had come through.

"Explains why the front is so quiet," Jessie said almost stealing Willow's exact thoughts. She nodded in agreement.

The main room was by far the largest with over double the space of the rest of the house. There were long tables and benches set up for eating at. Later, after dinner the children would move the tables and benches to one side of the room and find a spot on the floor for their pillows and blankets to sleep for the night. There were seventeen children that lived in the orphanage all between the ages of ten and fifteen, most had been under four cycles when their parents had been declared dead. They knew no other life than the one they were living.

All of the house inhabitants were in the main room, going over what looked like a long list of rules. The council had been coming down hard on the children lately for playing unsupervised outside and had threatened to, '*Put the whole lot to work keeping the castle clean if they had nothing better to do than pester people.*' That meant reduced outdoor time and strict rules for behaviour in the presence of others. The majority of the children were sitting on the floor in a semi circle around the adults as if it were story time. Off to one side, Willow noticed a boy leaning against the wall staring at her. He was short with brown hair and a few freckles or dirt spots, it was hard to tell which. His brown eyes held no emotion whatsoever and a long blade of grass hung out of his mouth to one side as he chewed on the other end. His clothes were old and patched over patches with some stains that would never come out.

"His name is Arnold," Jessie said braking the silence between them.

"I know, but shouldn't he be with the others?" Willow asked her gaze never straying from the sight of the boy.

"The new arrangements probably have him going stir crazy. It has to be rough hardly ever leaving this room," Jessie whispered.

Looking around the room she agreed that would drive her over the edge too. Still she couldn't help but feel there was something else behind that chilling stare.

Micca noticed them standing at the doorway. He hurried over to thank them both for bringing the food out to them and apologize for not meeting them sooner, then he excused himself to head back to his discussion with the children.

It was almost dinner time so they retraced their steps out of the building. Just walking outside it felt like a weight had been lifted from the air around them, so much more fresh and free.

Jessie, feeling the uneasiness in his friend offered, "Diana is having story time tonight. She asked me to tell you there is going to be something special she insists you need to hear."

Willow smiled all the way back to the market place. That was definitely the best news of the day and after the two parted, she headed home to clean up the mess for tomorrow and wash up for the evening's excitement.

Chapter Two

In the distance, sitting on a sightly higher elevation and to the north of the town, was the great castle made completely of different types of carved stones and metals with coloured glass windows. High peaks boasting elaborate statues of great majestic birds in flight enhanced the grandeur of the building. The large doors of the front entrance were big enough to allow way for a giant to enter and were elaborately decorated with a carving of a magnificent tree boasting beautiful sweeping limbs. On either side of the doors, stood two very large statues, the first of a large feline lunging forward and the other looked similar to a cross between a wolf and bear standing on two feet with arms outstretched and growling fiercely.

Inside, the carvings told stories like a picture book as they danced across the walls. Ask a question and the answer may be revealed or in the event of disaster, prophecies could be uncovered. The floors looked like polished marble with gold accents, lights twinkling above like stars in the ceiling. A grand stairway, in the middle of the room, twisted magnificently in a circular motion to the upper levels where the sleeping quarters were located.

There was enough space and living quarters to house more than ten times the town's population, but only council members, their families, the guards and some entertainers were permitted to stay anywhere on the grounds.

Looking to the right from the stairs, you could see two golden doors open wide to a glorious ballroom with a ceiling made of rare gems and crystals. Past that was a hallway leading to the dinning room which was decorated with crisp fine linen on tables set with fine porcelain dishes. Further down were food preparation rooms including a door to outside brick ovens for cooking. To the left of the stairs was a hallway which led to the common use rooms, mainly used for sitting and furnished with all the comforts one could hope for. Soft, golden coloured cushions lined every chair and grand vases filled with delicate flowers from the gardens, sat atop each of the beautiful brown polished marble tables.

At the end of the hallway were two blue, glass doors opening to a walkway, which led to an adventure through the gardens that tantalized the mind and offered utopia to the senses. Floral scents filled the air, a beautiful array of colours caught the sight and a sweet taste danced on the tip of the taste buds of anyone who was lucky enough to walk through. Stone benches and smaller versions of the statues out front added additional beauty throughout.

The path ended at a large iron gate. The highest point of the gate was a semi circular shape containing what appeared to be words '*E Pepvo Eco Glay Callum*' written in an ancient language that no one, currently living in the castle, could read or write. Malarchy had told people that the meaning was, '*The council above all others.*'

In the hours before sunset, a humming, musical in nature, whimsically arose from the garden as the beautifully coloured flowers of the day transformed into bright, glowing blossoms that lit up the pathways at night. The sun always set in the same place slowly disappearing behind the great hill, but not before setting it ablaze in a brilliant glowing green.

A stone wall surrounded the grounds with one iron gate leading into the property from the town merging with the path heading to the front doors of the castle. Four guards were always posted at the opening, two on each side, to ensure only invited people were allowed to enter. Behind the gates sat a building which housed the guards and entertainers. It was also made of stone with carved pictures of guards standing by open doorways, not like any of the doorways in the castle or the iron gates, but smaller with carved stones in each corner. In some of the pictures it appeared the guards were defending the opening from something coming through. There were twenty-six guards who rotated shifts covering the front gates.

They were permitted to send two people to town daily for food and other needs, for both the guards and entertainers, but other than that remained in the building unless called for by the council or on duty. At special events they were instructed to have extra guards inside the grounds to keep control at all times.

The entertainers were permitted to practice on certain days, at certain times and performed something different daily for the benefit of the council's amusement. They were not permitted to leave the castle grounds at any time. Any entertainer who disobeyed was not allowed back into the grounds and would have to return to their former life, which of course none of them wanted to do.

The grounds themselves were vast and included a practice area for all the different types of abilities, a courtyard for dances and events, and a games area for entertainment. The practice area had targets for shooting at, an obstacle course, an arts and crafts section, an invention studio, a stone patio, a grass area, and a fenced in area, and was mainly used by guards keeping their combat skills sharp and any entertainers preparing for a show.

The games area consisted of an outdoor arena where two or more people could test their abilities against each other. The arena had been closed for use for as long as anyone could remember. The courtyard was the most used area outside with a beautiful stone patio surrounded by stone benches for sitting. At the front was a stage type area where instruments and entertainment props were kept. Although there was a beautiful ballroom inside, the courtyard was the popular place to hold dances and other nightly entertainment.

During the daytime the younger children from the castle were allowed to play outside. They were rarely heard of or seen by the townspeople and never stepped foot outside the castle gates. The majority of times the youngsters were in a common use room away from everyday activities. At most large events, they would be paraded around for their cuteness factor, giving their mom's and dad's a chance to beam with pride over their little bundles of perfectness. This didn't always have a good effect on the older children who, occasionally, would become jealous over the toddler spot light. In particular, Jade wished many times her younger brother, Jordan, would go away or disappear, so that she would never see him again and she could have the full attention of her parents, mostly her mother, again.

Just outside the garden gates sat a large stone table and chairs where, almost every evening after dinner, the council would meet to discuss current events, business, if any, and laws. There were six chairs on each side and one at the end. A giant glass bowl of water sat in the middle of the table.

The council itself was made up of thirteen people and although they were all deemed to be equal, Malarchy and his wife Nebulah clearly lead the meetings and decisions.

"Old business?" Malarchy's voice rang out over all of the small talk going on at the table as the council members took their places for the meeting. He had claimed the single spot at the end of the table. Behind him the glow of the sun setting beneath the great hill illuminated his head and face in an eerie green aura, adding to his illusion of power over the rest of the council.

Malarchy was one of the oldest on the council although he looked no older than thirty. He wasn't remarkable by appearance standing at 5'10' with a slim build. His head was shaved bald and his teeth were uneven creating the appearance of fangs when he spoke or smiled. He dressed flamboyantly in fine linens of bright colours with golden trim and gemstones adorning every place possible. Most of the town weren't sure exactly what his abilities were and were too frightened to find out.

"None," replied his wife Nebulah to the left of him. She stood only 5' tall with golden blonde hair. Her most noticeable feature was the size of her chest, doubling the size of any other woman in town and matched with a small waistline and hips. It was a wonder she didn't lose her balance from being top heavy. Whenever she spoke a noticeably fake smile crossed her face directed at whomever her audience might be.

"New business then?" Malarchy's voice sounded again loud and confident.

"The children have asked we consider a dance to celebrate their sixteenth cycles," his wife answered immediately.

"We haven't for others before, why now?" argued Aurora. She was one of the newer members of the council and had been appointed only four cycles ago to the council as cousin of another council member Zebulon. Seated directly to the right of Malarchy, she was medium height but the thinnest lady around. As usual she was wearing a crisp white suit which was illuminated by the natural glow that radiated from her body. Her hair was short and spiked at the top with gold, silver and copper tones and her eyes shimmered the most electric hues of blues and purples. Unlike other council members she never felt the need to wear jewelry or to add anything flashy to her appearance.

Aurora was known as a *'light'*. She was able to read energies and she could lend energy to another person to enhance their natural abilities. Unfortunately, the lack of training for her talents meant she couldn't control them properly and would often misread an aura. Since large groups of people caused her headaches and pain, she hardly left her room except for some meals and daily council meetings and she avoided events and trips to town at all costs. Her lack of knowledge of her craft also meant she was a target for exploitation of her energy enhancing abilities and was rarely aware when someone was tapping into her energies, often left wondering why she would become very tired some evenings.

"There are an unusual amount of children this cycle who will be coming into their powers. Jade has suggest it may be a nice gesture and the girls are happy to see to all the details. I don't see any reason not to allow them a small celebration for their generation. Of course all of the castle will be invited to join in the fun," Nebulah rebutted.

"And the children from the town?"

Nebulah's face seemed to have to work a little harder to keep the smile while she answered. "Of course the boys of town will receive invites and can bring a date of their choice…There are a few young ladies who don't own a dress or know how to dance so we don't want to pressure them into something they may find uncomfortable to say the least."

Malarchy interrupted before anyone else could reply. "To vote then, in favour?" he counted the raised hands then added, "Against?"

Nine of the thirteen voted in favour, three against, being Aurora, Zebulon and Lynnea and one, Ozias, was asleep.

"A dance it is, but before the new cycle begins, so no unusual abilities arise at the dance I think is best." After a slight pause Malarchy added, "Is there anything else to discuss this evening?"

Zebulon stood and asked to speak from the other side of the table. He was a short round man, one could not deny that he enjoyed the bakery a lot more than the vegetables. He had brown curly hair and a full beard, well trimmed and tidy. His dress wasn't exceptional but he did adorn his fingers with rings of various gems, which he claimed aided him in his interpretation of the skies and the meanings of symbols and signs.

"I think we should revisit the prophecies."

The faces of all the others became stern and uneasy as each one turned and stared at the man still standing. Zebulon took his seat to wait for an answer, which didn't take long.

"We have dealt with the prophecies already," Malarchy snapped.

"I agree, we took steps to try to change the course of the future, but there are no longer any prophets left in our world to ask if we succeeded. What if we set in progress the fate we so desperately tried to avoid? Should we not take some action to prepare in case? Perhaps a Plan B, since we are talking about the complete destruction of our homeland."

Malarchy looked as if he was becoming more and more annoyed. Red slowly crept into his face as he answered, "Are you not the symbol interpreter? What do the skies say? The pictures on the wall?"

Zebulon's face looked solemn. "The wall has gone quiet. The pictures are gone and the skies offer no answers. The stars do not rise at night to form any signs, nor do clouds hold visions. I can no longer see anything pointing to any future."

Malarchy motioned to his wife to check the carved pictures in the walls inside the castle while the rest of the table sat quietly anticipating news. There was no smile when Nebulah returned and she simply nodded 'yes' to her husband who turned his attention back to the small plump man.

"And what do you suggest we do? We have no prophets anymore and now no symbols to interpret."

Staring down at his hands interlocked together on the table Zebulon replied, "We revisit the prophecies, look at them again, see if we can find any clues we may have missed and then decide on a plan of action should any of it still come true. Perhaps there is something we can change."

"And are you willing to answer questions which will arise as to the decisions the council made?" After looking at several council members each nodding, Malarchy added, "Very well then, Lynnea would you mind?"

Lynnea was Zebulon's wife and sat beside him at the table. She was what one might call mousey. Her hair was a dull grey which she unsuccessfully attempted to spice up with silver and crystal hair pieces. She looked awkward. Her clothes were always a bland colour, a shade of beige or tan and often untidy or buttoned in the wrong holes. She was shy and quiet, often not speaking a word to anyone except her husband and even then nothing more than whispers. She did, however, have an unusual ability which allowed her to take the minutes of every meeting. She could save pictures of everything she saw and replay them onto the face of water for others to see as well.

She nodded and stood directly in front of the large bowl of water. Looking directly into the bowl she raised her arms, hands wide open to the sky and the water followed forming a large cube over the table. After a few seconds, an image came into view on each of four screens of flowing water. It was a woman with long midnight blue hair.

The picture focused on the upper body and head. She was wearing what appeared to be a black uniform made for combat. The top was a sleeveless vest and on each of her arms just below the shoulder were pictures on her skin a single wolf on each side. She had a distressed look on her face which could have been construed as pure fear. The eyes of all council members focused on her face intently.

The woman began to speak with a bit of shakiness in her voice. "I have had a vision of the future our world is heading towards and we must take action. There is no time to waste. We have less than nine cycles before we are invaded by an army dressed in black and red, with weapons, the like of which I have never seen before, glowing swords, bows and guns of an unknown power source, hundreds of them, if not thousands."

"They are by far the most cruel, and strongest of enemies we have yet faced. There will be people murdered in the streets and others taken away as prisoners, stone statues crumbling and a storm in the skies as the weather turns deadly, with booms of thunder and lightening strikes more severe that I have ever experienced before. The gardens destroyed and the forest ablaze with fire. In the end nothing remains except for destroyed and deserted ruins. No life survives."

"We must fight this evil at its root before it destroys our very home and spreads its vicious will to all other worlds. Please consult the other seers and interpreters. Ask them to look into our future. I am scheduled to leave to aid Petra's expedition to the main world at sunrise. I have consulted with the guardians as to transferring some of my abilities to the walls of the castle for you to be able to ask guidance and to aid you in decisions. The changing pictures shall help you see what course your future is taking. Be strong friends and train as many as possible in my absence. The more who can fully use their abilities the better our chances for survival if the portal teams fail to destroy this threat before it reaches our home land."

The picture faded and the water fell back into the bowl. Lynnea returned to sitting. It was Aurora who spoke first. "Who was that? Was she a council member? Where is she now? Should we be worried?"

Malarchy looked at the council members again, rubbed his face and replied, "Her name is Iris and she was a council member in the guardian days of our world. After this prophecy, she did as she said and transferred some of her abilities to the castle walls, before she left the next morning to help in another world. Over the next cycle many teams were formed and deployed, to not only combat regular threats to the portals, but also to locate and stop this invasion from ever happening. After news of a battle gone wrong, all remaining guardians and trained teams left to aid the battle. A cycle past...none returned and no news had been received."

"The remaining council members decided to take action to protect the citizens left in our world. The portals to other worlds were disassembled and the parts destroyed so that no one could enter or leave. We then appointed new council members to replace those who were gone. In order to keep the population safe and calm and considering many had family members who gone to aid in the battle had not returned, we made up news of deaths. We implemented plans so people would forget and not discuss the past. I stand by the decision of closing the portals so that no malevolent force could ever use them against us, by entering our world and invading our sanctuary. The time of the guardians was finished, they would offer us no salvation. We were and still are, left to our own devices."

"If it was that easy, don't you think the others would have thought of that plan instead of putting their lives on the line?" Aurora was now showing signs of exhaustion, bags had formed under her eyes, her glow was dimming and her face had turned three shades whiter.

"I think we did the best possible. Leaving the portals open would have meant an unnecessary access point to our world for an invasion. Unless anyone else knows how an army could enter to attack us I don't see the problem."

Zebulon interrupted. "The problem is there are no signs to a future. We need to do something. Reinstate the training program and advance abilities so people can defend themselves if it does happen."

"Do you enjoy your life as it is now?" The tone in Malarchy's voice was showing signs of aggravation. "Do you think the good townspeople will not ask questions? Perhaps you believe they will understand the choices we made condemning their loved ones who may have still been alive?"

It was Aurora who rebutted. "Some of us were not involved in any of those decisions."

"Do you believe this life you have is because you deserve it. You are who you are because we made you that way. We gave you your seat on the council and your comfortable room in the castle. If you think for one minute people won't turn on you if the truth comes out, if the council loses control, or if people find out how strong some of their abilities really are, you are mistaken."

A confused look came over Aurora's face. "You mean our abilities aren't the strongest?"

Malarchy rubbed his temples and replied with a sigh in his answer. "You can't really believe glowing makes you powerful. You can hardly even read the energies you see and remembering pictures that you can play back in water is a nice trick, but hardly powerful, or Rowan's balls of light to see by, would hardly help in a fight."

Rowan darted a look of dislike at the speaker but remained quiet. He did after all only illuminate council meetings that ran late and nightly entertainment or events, with circular orbs of light.

"Each of you think about what you can do and what we know towns folk can do, great strength or speed, control of fire and ice, control of metals, to name only a few. We don't even know what some of the kids can do yet! Even with my powers of illusion and Nebulah's gift of persuasion we wouldn't be able to hold on to control. We would be overthrown, our families removed from the castle. The life we have would be over. Are you willing to give all this up for something which may never come true?" Malarchy said turning the charm back on.

In an unusual turn of events Lynnea offered, "There is a child who we know can heal, if her power was trained, if she had direction, she could save lives if there was a war."

"Do you believe that child will bother to save any of us after the way she has been ridiculed and after she finds out what happened to her aunt and uncle? Are you willing to take that chance? Or perhaps the young lad we have juggling at night for your entertainment learning how much more he can do with his mind, do you think he will thank you for the ridiculous outfits and exploitation of his abilities for your amusement?" Malarchy snapped back.

"No my friends, if we teach them more, enhance what they can do, they will turn on us. We will lose control. Perhaps we should vote. Now I don't want to be too hasty, let's give everyone a chance to think about the lifestyle we have and what could happen, what we could lose... for no reason. So the vote will be in the evening after the fourteenth sunrise from now, unless disaster strikes before then or more pressing business takes precedent."

"Until then look around, see how life could change not just for you, but for your families, your children. There is to be no talk of the meeting outside the council and we are each to go on as if none of this has been discussed...everything as normal. We will announce the sixteenth cycle dance to take place on the eve after thirteen sunrises, which should give the girls plenty of time to arrange everything and still be soon enough that we can implement any decisions after. Think hard, there will be no meetings until the vote unless emergency arises. Until then meeting adjourned."

The council members went there separate ways. The majority of them headed to the courtyard for tonight's entertainment, however, Aurora returned to her quarters, exhausted. Nebulah, Nyssa and Ashley went to find their daughters to discuss the plans for the dance and make up invitations. Even with all the gruesome talk tonight they were all still energetic and excited about the evening for their girls. It meant new dresses, new jewelry, new head pieces to adorn their hair. It meant shopping. Malarchy remained at the stone table for a few minutes collecting his thoughts, even with Aurora's energy boost he had been borrowing, he was far more tired than he had ever felt after a meeting.

His head was resting in his hands, elbows on the table for sometime, when he heard "Sir." He looked up to see a guard in front of him. He mused to himself he didn't even know the guard's name or if he even had a name.

"What is it?"

The guard replied, "A boy sir, at the gate, he says you told him to come speak to you if he heard anything."

"Bring him then."

The guards had been linked telepathically by the ancients to make it easier for them to handle emergencies. Now, however, they used this ability to send messages to save time. He closed his eyes and sent a message to his partner to bring the child up. A few minutes later another guard appeared with a boy walking beside him. As they drew near it became apparent the boy was Arnold from the orphanage. Malarchy had discovered the boy had a gift he could use, enhanced hearing and had offered the boy all of his desires for any useful information he might over hear by '*accident*'. He was curious as to the potential information so he dismissed the guards.

"You have something to report?"

"Yes, I overheard someone tell the girl, Willow, that Diana Waddington had a story to tell tonight, one that was very important that Willow hear," the boy offered.

"What is the story about?"

"I don't know sir. The story isn't to be heard till some of the children gather secretly at her house tonight after dark. I have never been to one, but I hear the stories run for a couple of hours. Can I move in now?"

Malarchy laughed. "No child, not yet. First I need to know this information is actually important. It will be dark soon. I want you to go and listen to the story and any other talk you might hear. Watch how Willow reacts. I need to know if there is a message for her and, if there is, if she understands it. Go now and report here tomorrow, then we can discuss your reward."

Chapter Three

Willow was so excited about the evening's scheduled activities she arrived early. Mrs. Waddington's house was always open and she never wanted anyone to knock since she never heard the knocking anyways. She opened the door and headed into the visitor's room where books lined shelves covering all the walls. There was one large chair which looked comfortable but worn where Diana sat to tell her stories, with numerous old pillows and blankets neatly stacked beside it. Later, the children would take them from the stack and settle into positions on the floor. In the corners of the room were four tall tables, just big enough for a couple of books, where people could stand and read. At one of the tables was Nathan.

Mrs. Waddington's grandson was twelve cycles and short for his age, although tall enough to read from books at the standing tables, with dark bronzed skin and golden brown coloured eyes identical to the colour his mother's had been. His hair was black with tightly woven curls, each one perfect.

The books on the table were closed and Nathan appeared to be studying the cover of one with some interest. His left hand moved over the book in front of him as if caressing it without actually touching it. Suddenly, a white light like a beam of energy exploded from the book to his hand. He closed his hand and smiled as if he was seeing utopia.

Willow moved forward watching his every move. Aware of her presence as she neared, Nathan looked up at her, the beam of light vanished and he gasped a little, "Please. Please don't tell anyone they can't know."

Confused she answered, "Know what? What are you doing? What was that light."

"I," he stuttered a little, "I was reading."

"But..."

Nathan motioned for her to stop by shaking his head back and forth while waving his hands in the same pattern. With a gulp he continued, "About a week ago, I was looking at the cover of a book and noticing the worn spots, where people had held the book in exactly the same place for so many cycles and then it happened this light appeared and within seconds I knew everything the book said, word for word, fully understanding it."

Willow smiled and moving closer looked between him and the book. She picked it up examined it and commented, "That's amazing! I wish I could do that. These stories are brilliant."

"No, no, you don't and I don't either. Gran, she would be heartbroken if she knew. She has such hopes for me to develop a useful ability. This, well if the council found out they would be less than impressed, especially since they don't want us reading books. They don't want us learning. I can't break her heart. She can't ever know."

"I still think it's great and don't want us learning is exaggerating a bit don't you think? They just don't want us using all our time reading stories instead of handling our daily duties is all."

She was cut off by him. "You really don't see," he said grabbing her arm. "I wish I could show you what I see."

Both her arm that he was holding and his, began to radiate a white glow. Willow's eyes opened wide as if they had never been opened before and were taking in a wondrous amount of sights to process. Then the glow faded, she picked up the book Nathan had been looking at and opened it, she knew the story, word for word, picture for picture, every detail. She could see images playing in her head the same as if Mrs. Waddington were telling it. She looked at him in amazement.

"I know this story, I can see it. You shared it with me."

His eyes starred back at her and he blinked a couple times and said, "Something new I will have to be careful of."

"But this is a gift you can share with everyone, you need to..."

She was cut off again. "No, I don't want anyone to know, now promise. Willow, please promise me you won't tell."

"I won't tell, but promise me, when no one is around you will show me more stories," she said looking at the second book. A perplexed scowl came over her face. "Nathan this book isn't written in any language I have ever seen before."

He took it from her, placed it in front of him and repeated the same process. Again the white light connecting hand to book appeared and a few moments later he smiled and said, "I understand it! Zoz ta'qu rogram! I understand it!"

Her eyes widened in disbelief. "Did you just speak a different language?"

"I did," he replied with a smile so big it took up most of his face. "Here," he offered and she extended her arm. The light bound the two again and when it was finished, her eyes darted back and forth as if they were trying to help process information.

"Amazing!" she blurted out "Zzz'hq!" She spun around in a circle, grabbed the boy and hugged him. "I can speak another language." Looking as if searching for information she added, "An ancient language used by only those who were

31

present at the beginning of our time. Do you know how incredible this is? And the story, the meeting between the guardians and the ancient snakes, the arguments over territory, over power, leadership, the need to be recognized as more important, stronger and better than subjects below them. It's riveting, compelling...treacherous yet beautiful. Do you think it's real, a history of sorts?"

"More likely a story, to teach a lesson about corruption, the good and bad in everyone, and choose the right path kinda deal. It's a big theme in many of Gran's books. But it's the oldest book here and it's not written in Gran's hand writing. I think it probably is a very old forgotten language, anyways it means we now have our own secret language, which is brilliant."

"Brilliant! This is the ultimate! Are you sure you don't want to share with others? I think they would be impressed from beyond." Willow could hardly control her excitement and spun around again.

"Yeah well you are a geek."

She stopped mid spin and turned to him. "I am not." The look on his face was disagreement. "Okay, I guess I am, a little," she added. "But you have to admit having our own secret language is exciting." She smiled.

The two moved away from the table just in time for the doors to open.

Diana Waddington always looked as if she had been royalty. Not because of fancy clothes or gemstones, but a true regal look about her face. Her hair was dark and always tied up in a bun, without a single strand out of place. She had naturally stunning features like no other in town. Her cheek bones were high, but with soft lines, her eyes a cool baby blue, spaced perfectly with long eyelashes leading to a small nose with a curved point at the end. Her lips were full and naturally red. When she smiled her teeth were pearl white, correctly spaced and sized. She was posture perfect with a straight back where ever she went and it showed off a beautiful figure with curves in all the right places...none too big and none too small. Diana always wore full length dresses in one solid pastel colour, always clean and crisp. There was no doubt she attended to her appearance daily in some ritualistic form. When she spoke, she pronounced every word clearly as if they formed off her tongue and lips perfectly. Her voice lifted and fell with emotion in all the right places, creating an almost musical tone.

"You two look like you are having fun. Continue on. I am just getting ready for tonight," Diana said.

In all the excitement, Willow had completely forgotten about the special story Jessie had told her about. She turned to Diana and asked, "What is so special about tonight's story? Jessie said you wanted me to hear it."

"Patience my child, you will hear it with others. Private readings might be construed as treacherous in some way by the council and I don't think either of us need to be considered as a threat by them, now do we?"

Diana had a point that couldn't be denied, so Willow and Nathan grabbed a pillow and blanket from the piles and chose a place to sit before the others arrived. Over the course of the next hour the others attending arrived. Jessie, Dezi, Pete, Victoria, Clairity, and Ashlyn chose the seats directly around them. Other children filled the remaining spots. There was the metal smith's son and daughter and two of the wood worker's daughters.

The boy in the corner caught Willow's eye. She nudged Jessie beside her and motioned towards the corner. It was Arnold the boy from the orphanage, and he had his eyes locked on her again.

"He must have heard us earlier when we were talking. I hope it's worth it because I wouldn't want to be him later when someone notices he isn't there," Jessie said.

Diana Waddington took her place in the chair. On the table beside her were candles with glass covers that illuminated the area perfectly for reading and a book, with a cover that was plain and a brownish red shade, covered with dust.

"Everyone, settle down and find a comfortable spot now. We are about to begin," she said blowing the dust off the book in a direction no one was sitting in and opening it to the first page. Silence fell across the room in anticipation.

"Once long, long ago, there was one world, which contained all of the different realms and every type of being or creature one could possibly imagine. There were small pixies whose wings would light up at night, no bigger than the size of your pinky finger and pointy eared elves dwelling in the trees of the largest forests, faeries who dusted the skies with playful magic and large ugly trolls who hid in the darkest caves of mountains, witches who could practice the best and the worst magic had to offer, half beast half man creatures with enhanced senses of sight and sound, mighty giants with one eye, goblins and gnomes, beings who lived under water, wizards and winks, dwarfs and men of all natures."

"Sitting in the middle, on top of a hill, watching over all, was an ancient tree named Acacia, taller by far than any tree that could be found, with beautiful green leaves on large drooping branches that gently swept the ground beneath them in the wind. She was one of the first ancients ever in existence. Together with guardians, she protected the right of each and every culture to exist and grow in its own way, in its own time and most importantly on its own path. Their purpose was not to judge what direction a realm chose to take, nor to involve themselves in regulating right and wrong for these realms, but rather to ensure that every type of creature in the realms had a chance to evolve on its own."

"You would not see the light if there was never any dark. Likewise, you could not distinguish what was right and just if there wasn't any wrong. All things are balanced."

"It wasn't long until another group of ancients with a darker side emerged comprised of beings, once considered guardians, who had chosen to act on impulse and desire rather than reason. They believed their powers made them better than the rest of the realms and that they should be treated as such, bowed down to, served and worshipped. A great battle began between the remaining guardians and those who had left the order to pursue personal gain and power."

"Realizing the battle was not advancing and that both sides would be bound in a stalemate forever, the Xiuhcoatle, a race of large serpents began a search that would change history forever. The snakes searched high and low for a weak man who could easily be manipulated, charmed with promises of wealth and power, to wage a war between the realms, so that the guardians would be forced to intervene. Apopp, one of the largest of the serpents, at long last found what they were looking for, a man named Adom and his wife Evila. They were mortal with no extraordinary talents, living a modest life. The couple were offered a drink of the blood of faeries, which Apopp promised would enhance their strength and speed and allow their family to claim other lands as their own and take riches for themselves. The two drank and war followed."

"They conquered many lands with the aid of the great serpent's potion. Within the realms, news of the benefits of drinking blood of the magical spread like wildfire and so did a new obsession with obtaining the power granting blood. Men began to try to conquer those who showed signs of magic in any form. Creatures were captured and persecuted, wars broke out, forests were burned, lives were lost and great kings obsessed with gold and riches were born, with one wish to extend their kingdoms and enslave those who opposed them. The blood wars were in full swing and such would be the theme throughout much of the world for some time."

"The remaining guardian races and Acacia decided they could not fight both the other ancients and protect the realms from each other. A decision had to be made and, after much discussion and thought, the one world was split by the realms into many different worlds with only portals left connecting each to the main world. For added protection, all portals required a guardian to activate them."

"The magical folk were safe again. The men were left to bicker and fight amongst themselves in their own lands. The power of the potions wore off and the ancient races were each given their own worlds to be bound to. The final decision was less than popular with many, especially a few of the kingdoms of men and the ancients."

"Before creating a land for themselves, the guardians chose a group of gifted and honourable beings to join them. There were many possible choices, but only so many could be chosen based on their disposition to act upon temptation and emotions that are within each of us. As a gift for their service, Acacia granted them and their families to come, the gift of extended life. They weren't immortal but without sickness or war they would live to the end of time and their age would not show, nor would their bones ache or body fail."

"A beautiful world was created with vast forests and gardens. A great house sat overlooking the rest of the world, a home for everyone. All were equal and all would train to ensure the safety of every being and to ensure only the guardians and their new friends had use of the portals. There could be no doorways into or out of the main world which could allow corruption to enter or leave."

"It was soon discovered that by creating the portals the guardians had to syphon off some of their powers and as a result they could not travel through the very gateways they created to the other worlds. They searched for a solution for many cycles. It wasn't until a young prophet suggested that the guardians might merge with another being, that one was found. Shortly after the prophecy rang true and certain men and women were able to merge with guardians as one. Two guardians was the maximum any one person could handle. In this combined form the guardians could pass through the portals and once on the other side the two could separate again."

"The arrangement proved to be advantageous in other ways as well. The host person could take on some of the guardian's traits, agility, balance, advanced perception, rear sight, tracking abilities and they could communicate in a telepathic form, with each other, while merged. There became three distinct groups now in this new home world, the guardians, the keepers and the guardian friends, all still treated equal, each with their own unique purpose in regulating the safety of all life."

"Teams were trained for their future adventures in the main world and different realms. They had many adventures over the cycles, but that is another story."

Diana Waddington used a piece of paper to mark her place in the book and placed it back on the table beside her. She looked up at the children who were stretching and starting to move off the floor. From the looks on their faces she could tell they were happy with the tale she had just told.

Jessie bumped Willow's arm as they were leaving. "So? What was so special you had to hear that story?"

"I don't know," she replied. "Maybe the whole good and bad in all of us thing, you know, the '*you are growing up don't murder anyone, it's just hormones kinda deal*'."

Jessie laughed. "I could see that."

"I did read a book earlier that mentioned the same races though. Do you think they could be real? I mean a race of evil snakes is disturbing to say the least and all that drinking of blood. Yuck. Who could do such a thing?"

"That's what makes the story so great." Dezi stuck his head between them and laughed. "You aren't scared of a little sensationalism are you? You sure you can handle being all alone tonight? Who knows what might find a doorway into our world and attack you. Now, if you need some company to keep you safe."

"Don't ask Dez cause you definitely wouldn't be safe!" Clairity laughed and everyone else joined in. The trio were dressed similar to each other tonight and had held the attention of several of the girls over the story for most of the evening. They were the three most eligible prospects for young girls looking for a future husband, including several girls living in the castle.

"I think if there was anything, including doorways to other worlds hidden in the forest someone would have found it by now. Think of all the times we have played hide and seek and never came across anything," Willow answered.

"No one has ever found where the forest ends though, so...who knows what could be out there." Pete smiled as he teased the girls.

"Okay, enough I am going to have night scares in my dreams." Clairity had a real sense of worry on her face and Willow understood the feeling, all the talk of monsters and blood was frightening, even if she wouldn't let the others see how she felt.

It was late and she had to be up earlier than the others so she turned to say goodbye and caught something out of the corner of her eye that stopped her dead in her tracks. It was Arnold and he was standing in the space beside the Waddington house, almost as if he were hiding in the shadows. She motioned again to Jessie who turned and looked. The boy backed up and started walking away as if nothing unusual had happened.

"He was watching us. It's a little creepy," Willow whispered to Jessie.

"That story really got to you didn't it?" He laughed. "Arnold isn't creepy. He is just another kid. Probably wanted to join in the conversation but was too scared of rejection. I think you should call it a night."

Willow agreed and uttered, "See you tomorrow," as she headed to her one bedroom shack for the night. Once inside she changed into her bed wear, laid down and pulled the cover over her head.

Closing her eyes, images of the story haunted her imagination. Sleep wasn't going to come easy, if she kept thinking about frightening things. She put the thoughts out of her mind and concentrated on the forest and its trees. The thoughts soothed her, made her feel better.

'Sleep child, you are safe tonight,' the female voice whispered gently and the world swirled around as Willow drifted off into a deep sleep.

Chapter Four

Willow could feel her breathe rhythmically moving in and out of her chest. A cool breeze brushed against her face. She opened her eyes to find herself standing in the middle of the town road. She was wearing a white silk nightgown which hung all the way down to her bare feet. Her hair was red and long blowing gently in time with her breathing.

A fog crept low to the ground, rolling in from the forest. She looked down as the eerie mist swirled around her ankles. In thinner patches, she noticed the ground was lined with faceless bodies, none moving. She headed down the street towards the tree line to see what she had thought to be fog was smoke. The forest was set a blaze in giant blue flames, everywhere. The clouds began to rumble with thunder and lightening lit up the sky as rain began to pour down on her. She tried to scream for help but she couldn't make any noise. Her mouth fell open gasping for words.

Her feet began moving, running aimlessly up the road. There was no other life...no signs of people. She approached the castle gates, but they were destroyed. Broken stone scattered throughout the grounds and only parts of the castle still stood amidst the rubble. The coloured windows were shattered, the stone table cracked in half. Disaster and destruction was everywhere.

There was nowhere to go. Then out of the blue she found herself running as fast as she could, climbing the great hill to the top. Sitting there was a tree, dying. She tried to help it, heal it, comfort it. A branch broke off hitting her in the head. She fell to the ground and watched as the rest of the tree burst into blue flames.

Willow tried to scream again, this time she burst out, "Help! Please someone help me!"

"Come towards my voice," she heard from a distance. Looking around she could see the face of her friend Ashlyn in what appeared to be a hole in the sky. A hand extended through the opening. Willow reached as hard as she could, finally grasping the hand. She felt herself being pulled up, escaping.

Like a jolt of electricity had hit her, she sat up straight in bed, sweat dripping down her face and her heart racing. *'It was a dream, just a dream,'* she told herself.

'What was it about child?' The male voice asked with concern.

'You don't know? I thought you were always with me,' she said.

'We can not enter your dreams, only a dream walker could do that. Dreams are for you and you alone. You can choose to share what happened with us and we can try to help you decipher the meaning if you would like.'

Willow went over the dream in her mind and decided, with the help of the voices, that the visions she had were just the result of her imagination playing on the story the night before. There was little time to linger over it, she had to prepare for the day, so she got up and dressed as usual and was surprised by a knock on the door. Answering it, she saw Ashlyn standing in front of her, still in her night clothes and holding on to a little rag doll as tight as could be.

She lunged forward and hugged Willow tight, as she burst out, "Are you okay?"

"You mean that was real? You were there? How?" Willow placed a hand over her mouth, her mind racing with questions.

Ashlyn shook her head. "I can't explain it. I have never gone into another person's dream before, just called my mom into a few of my night scares. It started about a month ago. The dreams are similar to the one you just had. Mom thinks they are a warning of some sort... of something that is coming, but we don't know what." She looked down at the ground. "They scare me, the bodies with no faces. Who do you think they are?"

"I don't know, people I guess, maybe from here, maybe from somewhere else," Willow replied.

"Can I stay with you today? I can help if you want."

Willow smiled. "Sure, but you will need to change into regular clothes first. We can meet back at the stands and sit together."

Ashlyn headed off across the street to change. Already behind, Willow began her daily ritual. She had just finished bringing the produce round front to the stands when her friend returned. After filling the stands the two girls sat down.

"So you are a dream walker." Willow said breaking the silence.

"I don't know what that is."

"You can move through the dreams of others and pull people into your own. It's a rare ability I bet." Willow added more apples to the fruit display in front of her.

"Yeah I guess," she answered with little enthusiasm. "Not what I would have chosen. I can't think of a situation where it would ever be helpful."

"You pulled me out of that night scare. Do you think you can die in your dreams? Could something have actually happened to me? You said the dreams were the same, do you know what happens next?" Willow sat down again her legs fidgeting.

"No," Ashlyn answered with a mouth full of berries. "I get to the same point, on the great hill when a branch falls and the dying tree catches fire and I call out, so mom pulls me out, the same way I did to you."

"Should we try to see the rest? You know see what happens?" Willow asked.

"No, I don't think that's a good idea, something bad could happen. I just wish it would go away."

The town's daily activities had commenced while the girls were chatting and, coming towards them, Willow could see Jade and her entourage as well as their mothers. The three girls had almost a skip to their walk and smiles that reflected the sun in such an intense manner, that they could make you squint from the brightness. The boys seemed happier the group was moving faster than normal. Nebulah, Nyssa, and Ashley strolled behind them, with a look of pride on their faces.

When Jade reached the produce stands she barked, "Just put together baskets. You should know what we like by now. We will be back in a bit." Without even stopping, she continued on.

"They are going to get new jewelry I bet." Ashlyn didn't take her eyes off of the girls until they reached the Shinning house and entered. "Aha, I knew it!"

Willow looked up from the baskets she was preparing just in time to see the group disappear into the house of the gem maker. Shortly after, Victoria emerged from the house and ran over to where they were sitting. She was still dressed in her sleep wear and looked as if she had left home in a rush. Normally, her long wavy hair would be neatly tied back in a pony tail or braids, but today it was loose and hadn't even been brushed.

"Can I join you? It's getting crowded at home," the young girl asked.

Ashlyn was quick to answer, "Of course you can. So what's going on over there anyways? Why the rush for new shinny stuff?"

"Something about a dance at the castle." Victoria was more interested in choosing something to eat from the fresh fruits in the stands in front of her than discussing details of some dance.

"A dance?" Ashlyn smiled. "Do you think we will be invited?"

Willow looked at her perplexed. "No!" she snorted. The two broke out into a round of laughter at the thought of Jade extending an invitation to them to join in anything.

A few moments later the council group emerged and swiftly moved to Ashlyn's house.

"I bet that's a lot of clothes they are ordering. Looks like I am going to be busy helping out for a while." The tone in her voice showed her lack of enthusiasm towards the task of making beautiful outfits for a dance she probably wouldn't ever see.

Two guards sent to town for supplies stopped at the stands and were looking over what was available. Faramund pointed at corn. From the corner of her eye, Willow noticed a picture on his lower arm, not like the ones she had which were life-like. Iskander, the other guard made a similar motion towards the grapes and peaches. The same image appeared on his arm. A scowl crossed her face. How she had never noticed before?

"What does that symbol mean? The one on your arms," she asked.

The two guards looked at each other and then at the girls all bursting with curiosity. Both guards were tall and muscular, Iskander's pale skin was so strikingly different from his friend Faramund's golden skin tone, that it made him look a distinctly paler white than he might have appeared if he was alone, combined with his fair hair colour and one could have thought he had been so frightened that the colour had completely left his body.

Faramund pulled his sleeve back revealing the picture to the girls. It was an oval shape with four swords, one representing each direction, north, south, east and west, tips meeting in the middle and was a deep blue colour.

"The oval represents a door, or..." he paused for a moment looking at the other man as if they were somehow discussing what to say. "A gate, with the four swords intersecting representing two guards on each side. The swords meet at the middle allowing no one to pass. Put simply it is a sign of our birth right to protect."

"So every guard has that picture?" Willow continued her interrogation.

"Yes," Iskander answered. "When chosen for service as a guard, the symbol will appear. It is a great honour to be given the responsibility."

"If I wake up one day and have the same symbol, I would just be a guard?"

Both men laughed. "Something like that, but guards are appointed based on need, and there hasn't been a need for new guards in a very long time," Faramund replied.

"Does that mean something would have to happen to one of you for another to be needed?" Ashlyn's asked with a mouth full of berries, a red ring forming around her lips from the decedent juices.

"I hope that doesn't happen, but, it is a way in which a new guard could be needed. The most common way still is an increase in the number of... gateways that need protecting," Faramund replied.

"In other words, a new guard won't be appointed unless there are not enough guards alive or available in relation to number of gateways needing guarding," the other man offered.

As interested as Willow was to continue the conversation with the two men, Jade and the others were emerging from the ordering their new clothes. She had no desire to be on their bad side or get anyone else in trouble, so she thanked them for the conversation, handed them their baskets and they were on their way to the baker's when the council group picked up their orders. As suspected no invitation to the dance was extended.

The rest of the day was dreary. Victoria returned home. The whispers in the line of who was invited and who wasn't was too much for Ashlyn, so she headed home to help her parents. Since very little happened on a daily basis, the dance was going to be the hot topic for the next couple weeks until the event was over. Willow herself was glad when it was time to drop off food to the orphanage.

Dezi came over to help with the delivery today. He was fun to be with, quick with the jokes and always made Willow smile. All the way there she managed to avoid the dance topic. She already knew that the brothers had been invited and in her opinion there was nothing to discuss.

Micca was waiting for them out front so the two wouldn't have to go inside. Willow couldn't help but wonder if this may have had something to do with Arnold sneaking out the night before.

The way back was unusually quiet almost awkward. A couple times it seemed that Dezi was going to start to say something but changed his mind. He would sigh, rub his hand through his hair, then shove both hands in his pockets before continuing the walk. They were about half way when he came to a complete stop.

"So, I guess you heard about the dance?" he said, his voice cracking. He swallowed and coughed.

Just the topic she had hoped to avoid. Holding her breath a little she answered, "Yes, I wasn't invited though." There was a silent pause for a moment before she added, "I am sure you will have a great time. Everyone is talking about it. The biggest event in forever."

"Yeah it sounds great. Thing is no girls were invited," he replied kicking the dirt beneath his feet.

"How can you have a dance with no girls? Sounds rather awkward," Willow said starting their walk again.

He laughed. "Well, the guys were given an invite for two. We are supposed to bring a...date," he said matching her pace.

"Oh, I get it. Have you decided who you want to take?"

Dezi stopped walking abruptly. "I am trying to ask you," he blurted out.

"Me?" she squealed out in shock. "I thought Jade or one of the other council daughters." She looked down at a few pebbles on the ground. "Are you sure?"

"Jade is pretty to look at, but I would have a much better time with you. You know when to laugh and don't ruin my jokes," he said winking at her with a twinkle in his eye.

She let out the air she seemed to have been holding through the whole conversation. "I can't dance. I might hurt your feet, but if you still want me to go with you, I will."

"Excellent!" The two returned to walking. "See you later," he added as they approached his house.

Willow felt as if she was going to burst if she didn't tell someone the news soon. She was going to the dance. As soon as Dezi disappeared inside, she changed her direction to find Clairity and Ashlyn.

She found her friends in a quiet spot under a tree in the forest. The girls beamed of enthusiasm as they listened with excitement to the story. They all simultaneously let out a little yelp, which someone walking by might have considered a hurt animal.

"Can you believe it? Me going to the dance. I have never been invited to anything in my life. It's the most amazing feeling," she said grabbing Ashlyn's hands and spinning round in circles.

Clairity smiled at the two. "I can't wait to see the look on Jade's face when she finds out."

Willow stopped in her tracks and sat down. "I forgot about that." The smile faded from her face. "What was I thinking, Ohhhhhh...Why did I say yes? I can't dance and I have no dress and Jade is going to cut me into pieces. I have to tell him I can't." Panic was setting in.

"No," Ashlyn said. "Why should she ruin your fun."

Clairity agreed smiling. "She is right. You need to do this for all of us wretched folk who won't be invited."

"You don't know that. There are lots of boys that got invites for two." After a pause she added, "What am I going to do? It's a disaster."

Ashlyn smiled. "A little dramatic don't you think? Come on." She motioned for her friends to join her. "Let's go."

"Where are we going?" Willow asked.

"To my house. You will see."

The three headed back to Ashlyn's house. The front room of the house was filled with different fabrics, cushions, and finished clothes as well as standing figures with dresses in the process of being made. Down the hallway to the right was her sleeping quarters. It was more comfortable than a typical family would have. There was a body cushion on her bed and open cupboards filled with different types of clothes.

"Let's try some of these on," she said motioning to Willow while removing a handful of dresses from her closet.

After trying on dress after dress, it became apparent that their figures were not compatible and there was no way any would fit her.

"Thanks for trying."

"What are you girls doing in here," Ashlyn's mother asked peaking in the doorway. "Oh my, dress up time?"

The girls explained the story to her. The whole time her face seemed to hang on every word with excitement. "One of our own going to a dance at the castle. It's about time I say. Oh this is good news. These dresses won't do, no not at all. Ashlyn fetch me me bag. We'll make you a new dress. You will be the belle of the ball after I am finished."

Seconds later, Ashlyn was back with a tapestry bag filled with tapes to measure with, pins, needles, thread and a sketch book with notes and designs. Martha immediately started to measure, standing on the bed to reach Willow's chest, shoulders and arm span. After each measurement she recorded information in her book and added an "Ahuh" or "Aha". The whole process only took a few moments and the seamstress looked deep in thought. "Hmm," a slight pause. "If only we knew what colour your hair would be that night so I could pick something that wouldn't clash."

Without thinking Willow added, "Red." She wasn't sure why, but she was thinking back to the dream. Her hair was a deep warm brown right now.

"Don't be silly child," Martha said smiling. "No one has had red hair in ages and I doubt that is going to change any time soon. I think black might be the best choice for the dress. It goes with everything. Don't you worry about a thing. You will have the finest dress I have ever made. Now off you girls go and stay out of my hair while I work."

Martha had been the closest thing to a real mother Willow had ever had. She was short, a little plump, with short curly black hair and always wore floral print dresses with a white frilly apron over top. She never felt like she was assigned a job. She loved to sew. No one knew how exactly she made the material she used. Her *'trade secrets'* was the answer she would give if anyone asked, but it had something to do with leaves, flowers, broken branches from trees and weeds. On numerous occasions the girls had gone into the forest to gather various *'materials'* for her.

"Maybe gather some wildflowers from the forest for me over the next few days if you have nothing better to do," Martha added.

The girls agreed and headed outside still bubbling in excitement over the dress so much that they almost bumped into Mrs. Shinning trying to go inside.

"Oh Willow darling, are you getting a dress and shoes? Dezi told us you two are going together. It's so exciting isn't it! Don't you worry about a thing. We will take care of all the details. Mr. Shinning just wanted to know what colour you would be wearing."

"Black, I think, but I really don't need anything too fancy. I am not sure I would feel comfortable," Willow answered.

"Don't be silly. We have already started designing a couple pieces for you. You two will be the couple to admire," she said closing the door to the seamstress's house behind her.

"What have I got myself into?" Willow asked her two best friends. Looking behind the two, she saw a boy walking towards the castle gates. "Is that Arnold? What's he up to?"

The two girls spun around and watched the boy moving at a quick pace out of sight.

"He is probably going to try to ask someone at the castle to the dance," Ashlyn offered, trying not to snicker at the thought of Arnold on a date with Jade.

"Yeah maybe," Clairity responded still staring down the road. She had a half scowl on her face that indicated she didn't believe that answer, but wasn't going to offer an explanation. After a few moments she added, "We should get some rest. I have a strange feeling something big is going to happen tomorrow." She looked at her friends faces and continued, "It's just a feeling. I don't know what exactly, but my intuition has been bang on the past while."

The three hugged.

"Goodnight and happy dreams," Clairity said with a half smile. "And guys, stay away from Arnold, I feel all kinds of bad vibes coming for his direction. I know it's weird but please, just tell me you will."

The two girls agreed.

Chapter Five

It was already getting dark when Arnold arrived at the castle. Approaching the gates he addressed the guards, "Take me to Malarchy and make it fast. He won't want you messing around with me standing here waiting."

The four guards exchanged glances and a smirk before Eudard took the assignment and headed off to see if the boy could enter or should be turned around and sent home as a nuisance. To his surprise upon finding Malarchy, he actually agreed to see the boy. Using the guards' natural telepathic connection he sent a message to the others to escort the child into the garden area.

Arnold wasn't even in front of the self declared council leader when he blurted out, "I have the information."

Malarchy glared at him and motioned to the two guards. "Wait outside the garden gates. This won't take long." After they left, he turned his attention to the boy. "Do not address me in public unless I have indicated I want you to speak again. Are we clear?"

Arnold held his gaze as if he was not backing down, then the edges of his lips curled upward just a touch. "Fine, just as long as you remember our deal. I have information and I want what's coming to me."

"And you will get it and so much more, as long as the information is something I can use and you remember your place. So spit it out. What is so important that you are out after dark."

"This is the only time I could escape after the other day. Those people don't know who they are dealing with, yet," the boy snarled.

"Yes, yes boy, time is precious, let's get to it," Malarchy said.

"The writer, Diana Waddington's story, I went and listened like you asked. It was about ancient races, guardians and Acacia a giant tree. Sounded to me like she was hinting the tree used to stand on the great hill. It was quite the story, with portals to different worlds and wars. Even included drinking of blood. Pretty sure the girl didn't understand any message from it though. Not sure that group is bright enough to understand much."

The colour drained from Malarchy's face. "Very well we will look into it, now away with you."

"No, we have a deal. I am not going back to the place anymore. I want a room here, tonight, and to be treated as one of you," Arnold barked back.

"Who do you think you are talking to?" Malarchy snapped grabbing the boy's arm and dragging him towards the garden gates. "You will do what I say, when I say and right now I say you will go back to town as if nothing has happened. After I check out your tale, I will decide what it's worth to me and not a second before. Do you understand me?" Without waiting for an answer, he added, "Good." Then he turned the boy over to the guards with instructions to remove him from the grounds and send Zsiga to the gardens.

It took less than a minute for Zsiga, the head guard, to reach the stone table where Malarchy had taken a seat. His skin, hair and eyes were all dark allowing him to move in the shadows with ease, especially at night, one of the skills which had help him obtain the position of leader over the other guards. His impressive muscular build was another. "Sir, you sent for me?" he asked.

Malarchy seemed to be off in deep thought. He looked up and answered, "Yes, yes I did. Get together a team of men. There is something that must be done to protect the greater good of our citizens. I will meet you at the main gates with instructions in two hours. Make sure your men are prepared with weapons ready and lit torches." He dismissed the guard and moved inside the castle where he stared at the blank wall silently until it was time to give his instructions.

Chapter Six

Willow sat up straight, and took in a deep breath. She must have been dreaming again she told herself. It was hours still before she had to get up, so she laid back down and had just closed her eyes again when she heard a scream from outside. This time she knew she wasn't dreaming and she jumped out of bed.

'What are you doing? Where are you going?' The female voice seemed alarmed. *'Stay inside. You don't know what is happening out there. You could get hurt.'*

"Sounds like someone else is hurt. I need to try to help," she said out loud. Truth was she was scared and wasn't sure who she was trying to convince the voices or herself. Things had been changing so fast lately. Her life had become a mystery she needed to solve. She opened the door and stepped into the street.

'Go back inside!' The voices were louder now, upset. *'You aren't even dressed. Someone could see.'*

Willow didn't even hear the voices. She was stunned at the sight of guards piling books from Diana's house on to a big bonfire in the middle of the street. There was one guard on each side of the house stopping people from getting close. Diana was being held by her arms by two guards on the front porch. She was screaming and crying. Nathan was curled up on the side of the porch. Without thinking she ran towards him. Nathan, seeing her moving toward him, got up and met her at the edge of the porch just as a hand grabbed her shoulder from behind.

It was Faramund the guard she had been talking to earlier that day. He pulled her back into the shadow between the two houses. "You shouldn't be out here girl," he said. He turned his gaze to the boy still holding on to Willow's waist. "He doesn't need to see this take him to your home, you can't help the woman now." He removed his jacket and put it over her shoulders. "Quickly now, before anyone else notices, the council would be far harder on you than they will be on the storyteller if they find out." He moved out of the shadow and back to his post.

Willow looked down and realized she was wearing her night dress. It was white and sometimes hung off one shoulder. Suddenly, she understood. Faramund had seen the pictures on her back...he was helping her. As the guard had suggested, they ran across the street back to her room where she had the boy turn around so she could change into clothes that covered everything.

She didn't understand what was going on, but she had a feeling she knew who did. She had Nathan lie down and try to rest, then took a position as if she were meditating and called out inside her head, *'I know you can hear me. I think it's time you told me what is going on.'*

'When it's time we will. You have to understand, there are things you must discover on your own. Unless you are in direct danger.'

Willow cut the voice off. *'Danger, you don't think what is happening to Diana is danger?'*

'A dangerous situation perhaps, but it doesn't impose direct danger to you and that is our concern. What is happening here is wrong, but you can't fight it alone and defiantly not before you mature to your full potential. Until that time you must be patient and trust us.'

She stood and moved to the door. Opening it a crack, she saw the guards taking Mrs. Waddington towards the castle, with her hands bound in rope behind her back. Willow looked back at Nathan on the bed, *'People are getting hurt. How can I do nothing when I know they would do everything for me?'*

'You are more special than you know, others see that,' the male voice responded to her alone.

She left the door slightly open and backed up to the wall, sliding down to a sitting position, and watched the fire burning all the books she loved so much. Tears swelled in the corners of her eyes until she could no longer handle the burning. She cried.

At the same time, rain started to pour down, harder than she had remembered it ever raining before. Within minutes the bucket on her table was already over flowing. She sat, tears racing down her cheeks, watching the rain turn the fire to smoke, oblivious to everything else.

Clairity ran across the street and knelt down to her. "What are you doing? It's late. The council will be in town anytime now and the stands are empty."

Willow looked at her and replied, "It's still raining. I never start work till the rain stops."

"It's been raining for hours. No one knows why. It's never happened before. Come on I will help you," Clairity offered.

The two girls decided to leave Nathan in bed agreeing he needed the sleep and headed out back. Willow was feeling better with a friend to lean on. The rain was starting to let up. She didn't even notice when it stopped completely. She had been too absorbed in getting the stands filled, telling herself people counted on her and she couldn't let them down.

Four guards came to her stand, two picking up the council's needs because of the unusually wet weather and the other two attended to the needs of the guard house. After they left, people darted from their houses picking up essentials and hurried home again. Even when the sun was shining again, no one lingered outside and talk was short without eye contact. People were scared.

Ashlyn joined her friends behind the produce stands. "Where do you think they took her? I hope she is okay," she said sitting down, with a blank stare on her face.

The other two girls looked at her both placing one finger in front of their lips, motioning for her to be quiet. "Nathan is still sleeping inside," Clairity explained.

"Sorry," Ashlyn whispered back.

"It's okay, I am up," Nathan said from the door. He moved over and sat down, staring across the road at his grandmother's house and the remains of charred books in the middle of the street.

Sometime had passed in complete silence when Ashlyn motioned for the others to look up. Jade, Camile and Sabrina were almost skipping by like nothing had happened. They headed straight to Ashlyn's house, most likely to check on their orders.

It was only a few minutes later that the girls emerged, Jade slamming the front door. Just from looking at their faces one could tell they were not happy about something. Jade practically stomped over to the Shinning house with the other two trying to console her about something. Martha appeared in her doorway and motioned for her daughter to stay where she was. Seconds later everyone in town would hear Jade let out a blood curdling scream. People were peaking out their windows and doors at the Jewelry maker's house trying to catch a peak at anything they could see.

Jade emerged from the house yelling. "I'll be back with others, don't think you'll get away with this." She stormed down the street back to the castle, her two friends running behind her.

"What was that about?" Nathan asked.

"Not sure," Clairity replied. "But I have a feeling we need to stay here, this isn't over yet."

The four of them continued making baskets for people as they sporadically appeared. It was about an hour later when they were packing up the remaining food that Jade returned with her mother and headed straight to the Shinning place. They could hear an argument but couldn't make out the words. It lasted for about ten minutes, then Nebulah and Jade emerged and walked to the dressmaker's house. This time Nebulah motioned for her daughter to remain outside. Jade stood glaring in Willow's direction while waiting. Again an argument could be heard but they didn't know what it was about. When Nebulah returned to her daughter they had a few words and Jade raised her voice, "I don't care. I want them and I will have them. They are making fools of us mother and you are letting them." Jade stormed off back to the castle her mother walking slowly behind her.

Willow was starting to head over to the Jewelry maker's house when Martha ran out and sent her back. "Not now, let this settle. We can handle it. You four just deliver those boxes and call it a night. Get some extra sleep." She handed Willow an extra blanket and pillow for Nathan and turned to go back inside.

Willow was glad the group did as suggested. After the night before, she was exhausted and fell right to sleep.

Sometime during the night the pile of burnt books had been removed from the road. All that was left the next morning was a black spot on the grey and brown path where the fire had been. Willow attended to her normal duties trying to start the day as if nothing had happened. It was impossible to not see something was going on. Her beliefs were confirmed when the council sent guards for their daily needs again. Nathan had suggested perhaps the council realized they could do less if they made the guards do daily errands for them. Having a giggle together was the highlight of the morning for the two. The day stretched on with people hurrying to get their food and trying to avoid talking.

She wondered how long they would live like this, scared to interact with each other. Suddenly to her surprise Jade appeared in front of her.

"Do you really think you can be anywhere near better than me. This is a warning to you. I will get what I want no matter what it takes. I'd move aside if I were you before you or your friends get hurt." Jade flip her hair as she turned and headed towards her home.

Willow took a moment to process what had just happened. Had Jade really just threatened her? Why? What had she done? It was time to go for a visit and find out.

She opened the door to the Shinning house and walked in. Augusto Shinning was working on what looked like a necklace. He was a funny looking little man with pure white messy hair that could have used a cut and a big white moustache which curled up at the ends. He looked up at her and called for his wife.

"Opaque, we have company." He stopped his work and smiled at her. "How are you today Miss Willow?"

She wasn't sure how to answer. Under the circumstances it almost felt like a trick question. Luckily she was saved by Mrs. Shinning.

"What a lovely surprise, does Dezi know you are here? I can call him."

"No thank you," Willow said, her voice shaking a little. "I came to see you."

"Oh," Opaque replied. "What can we do for you my dear?"

"Well," she said thinking about her words for a second before deciding to just tell them out right. "I had a visit from Jade today, she was angry at me for something I am not sure I understand. I saw she had an argument with you as well and I wondered if it was in some way connected."

Augusto took a deep breath in and let it out slowly. "I am afraid it is the things some people in town are making for you to go to the dance. Jade decided she wanted them for herself and when we refused to give them to her she became enraged."

Willow had a look of horror on her face. "I don't want to be the cause of any arguments. Please make the items for her so she will be happy."

"No my dear, it doesn't matter if we give the things we are working on to her. The second we make you something else she would want that too. Greed has overtaken that girl. The town all agreed we would not give in. The items we make for you, will be for you. Don't worry about Jade she will have to get over it. Now head on home and put it out of your mind."

She did as he requested and headed back across the street. Ashlyn met her part of the way.

"Guess they told you huh."

Willow nodded and retold the story of Jade from earlier.

"That's terrible. She actually threatened you and your friends?" Ashlyn looked astonished. "I wouldn't worry. What can she do? Her parents aren't about to take on the whole town."

It was the next day when Jade and her mother returned again. This time she was carrying something in a hand basket and her two girlfriends, Camile and Sabrina, were on either side of them. They headed straight to the Shinning house again. Jade and Nebulah entered and the other two stood outside. They looked ridged, nervous almost. Sometime passed before mother and daughter appeared again. Whatever Jade had been carrying was gone and they entered the seamstress's house. This time all four went in and emerged a few minutes later. As they moved across the street Willow could see Ashlyn in her doorway. She shrugged her shoulders before her mother closed the door.

Jade stepped forward smiling. "I am sorry for the way I acted. I hope you will forgive me. I am sure we can be friends and we can't wait to have you come to the dance."

Willow was almost in shock. "Thank you," was all she could manage to say.

They headed back to the castle.

*'What was that?' s*he asked with her inside voice.

'Trust your instincts,' was the answer she received.

Martha and Opaque both crossed the street to see her.

"See! We knew no parent would allow their daughter to act like that," Mrs. Shinning smiled.

"Everything is fine now and you will have a wonderful time at the dance," Martha added placing her arm around Willow's shoulders and squeezing.

"I suppose," Willow still wasn't sure. "If you don't mind me asking what did Jade bring you?" she asked Mrs. Shinning.

"Not me dear. She felt bad for the way this affected Dezi and his brothers. She wanted to make sure they still attend the dance so she made them a small cake. The four of them enjoyed it together while the adults talked about designs for the council girls."

Willow couldn't imagine Jade baking anything. But over the days leading up to dance, she came everyday with a baked cake for the three boys.

The days and nights had been relatively uneventful and went by quickly. Then the dance day was upon them. Everyone was busy preparing last minute details.

Ashlyn, Nathan and Clairity had agreed to run the produce stands for the day so Willow could get ready. She was nervous and glad that Mrs. Shinning and Mrs. Needle were going to help her. The two ladies showed up and uncovered the most stunning dress and jewelry she had ever seen. They stepped outside while she slipped into the dress.

It was pure black and started with a collar around her neck attached to two straps that went down the front attaching to a sleeveless, backless top. It connected at the waist to a skirt that reached the floor. There was a gold chain that ran from the collar at the back to the top of the skirt at her waist. Suddenly she remembered the pictures. She stretched to look at her back. There was nothing there. Puzzled she continued looking until she heard a giggle. *'Alright you two, where did the cats go?'*

She received her reply right away. *'To your stomach.'*

'They can move? Why didn't you tell me?' She was quite upset.

'Relax, it's new,' the other voice said calmly. *'The further you go into your sixteenth cycle the more changes will happen.'*

Martha peaked her head back in the door, "Can we come back in? Oh you look beautiful." The two ladies walked in without waiting for an invitation.

"Stunning," Opaque added. "Your hair, it's...red," she added looking at the seamstress. "I haven't seen that colour in a very long time."

The two ladies helped Willow fix her hair up off her neck with a few wispy strands flowing down around her face, then put on the earrings, necklace and hair pin that had been designed just for her.

It was time to practice walking in the shoes. The two women had her walk back and forth until she could walk without toppling over, something Willow thought was the hardest task she ever had to do. In the end it wasn't perfect, but on the arm of a strong guy she could get through the night. Confident they had done their best, the two mothers left, heading home as did Willow's friends. Nathan was staying at Ashlyn's for the night so there was nothing to interrupt the evening.

Clairity came over a few minutes later. "Wow you look amazing."

"What are you doing here?" she asked.

"I had a feeling you might need some company," Clairity replied.

"Right again," Willow said. "I am nervous. What if I make a fool of myself, or fall down or..."

"Don't be silly," her friend interrupted. "You will be brilliant."

The two girls sat and waited. The sun had gone down and, from where they were, the girls could hear the music from the dance.

"He isn't coming is he?" Willow said more as a statement than a question. Her eyes glancing down at the ground.

"Maybe something happened. You don't know for sure. He wouldn't just not show up. You two are good friends." Clairity turned around seeing that her friend wanted to change out of the pretty dress she was wearing. "You could wait a bit longer."

Once back in her own clothes, she handed the dress, shoes and jewelry to Clairity. "Would you return these for me? I am sure someone will be able to put them to good use." She said her hands shaking.

Clairity agreed not knowing what to say or do. She could see the pain in her friend's face... the way she was straining not to cry. Reaching out she touched her shoulder. That was enough to make Willow bolt, running as fast as she ever had before, disappearing deep into the forest.

Clairity for once didn't want to listen to her intuition. It was telling her to leave Willow alone for now, that she would be fine and this was how things needed to be. She hadn't been wrong since developing the ability and hadn't questioned it once till now. In the end she decided to let her friend have space for the rest of the night and she headed across the street to return the items and share the sad story of the evening's events.

Chapter Seven

Willow slowed her run to a walk and then stopped bending over to catch her breath. She had been running for sometime, not thinking, not listening, just running. She looked around and realized she had ended up near the castle wall. Climbing one of the largest trees she had a bird's eye view of the courtyard.

The music was still playing, couples were dancing, twirling in time to the beat, while floating balls of light lit the sky above sending a gentle glow down on the festivities. To one side, a man in a bright red and orange suit was juggling three spheres of fire with his bare hands and every so often a lady dressed in shimmering silver and gold would motion upwards to the sky following which sparks of glitter would rain down from high above in pretty patterns. Those lucky enough to be in attendance were all dressed in fancy clothes, beautiful flowing dresses and crisp suits. It was more beautiful than she had imagined. Her eyes stung with held back tears.

'First love is always the hardest, time will heal.' It was the female voice she had become so accustomed to over the years trying to console her...worried about her.

Willow sighed. *'It isn't love. Dezi is a great guy and a good friend, but I don't think I even know what love is yet. I hear other girls talk about a single touch sending shivers down their spines, their thoughts filled with one person, one face. Truth is I haven't felt anything even remotely close to what they describe. No, it's my pride that is hurt. I wanted to be there... to be good enough to be there. I wasn't and Jade was right. She won and it leaves me feeling defective in every way possible.'*

'We are proud of you, few of your age could see the difference.'

'That doesn't help how I feel right now,' Willow responded. As a single tear trickled down her face storm clouds filled the sky and, as if feeling her sadness, the clouds wept with her and rain began to fall over the castle grounds. "Did I do that?" she asked out loud.

"Yes," seemed to whisper on the wind. This time it wasn't a voice she had heard before but yet was somehow familiar. She looked around expecting to find someone had followed her from town, but there was no one.

"Who said that?" she demanded.

"We did," was answered.

She slid part way down the tree with ease, never losing her footing. She never did. For as long as she could remember she had been climbing the highest trees and swinging from branches without ever falling once. She placed one hand on the trunk of the tree she was in and realized it was the trees who were speaking to her. She could hear them whisper to her. The leaves rustled words of pleasure she could finally hear them. As they swayed in the breeze, they sang to her as a mother sings to a child.

"Trees? Am I talking to trees?" She slid further down towards the ground.

"Yes, you always have, you just didn't realize it until now. Since the first time you climbed up on our limbs as a young child and almost fell. You called out for help and a branch steadied your feet beneath you. Through the years, we have shared your most intimate feelings. When you were sad, you came to us and we cradled you. When you were mad, we listened to you. When you were happy, we danced with you."

Willow thought back and remembered. It was true. Whenever anything happened in her life she would go to the forest, climb the trees, run across the branches, sit secure on the tallest limbs. There she felt safe, protected, loved.

She slid down to the ground and realized she hadn't been climbing at all. A branch beneath her was lowering her slowly to the base of its trunk. She muttered a *'thank you'* and began walking without direction. There was so much to think about, to let soak in. So this was her ability...what she could do.

'Partly, there is still so much more if you choose to learn,' the familiar female voice returned.

'Are you a tree too?' she asked.

She heard laughter all around. *'No, we are not,'* the male voice answered.

She was about to ask another question but up ahead she saw something she had never seen before. She quickened her pace to a clearing around a building made of white stone with intricately designed columns and a flat top. There were no doors, but rather steps on both sides leading up to an open platform with a table in the middle. On either sides of the platform were round semi circular shaped rooms with carved shelves lined with books.

Stepping inside, the structure seemed far bigger. There were thousands of books, more than she could ever imagine reading.

'What is this place?' she asked.

'Home to the keepers,' the male voice answered.

"Keepers? As in guardian keepers, like in the stories?" she asked out loud. A shiver in her voice let on she was almost afraid of the answer she would get.

'The stories are true, every bit, every part. Diana has an unusual talent of recording history in writing and teaching it to others. She was the official

historian of our world and used to teach past events in school at the castle. The books here are references keepers felt necessary to keep protected. Some contain the different abilities of every living person in this world, others with maps and languages of all the different worlds. Every question you want to ask, the answer is here.'

"Why haven't I seen this place before? Or anyone else I know for that matter." She was astounded by her find.

'Only a keeper or someone led by a keeper can find it. The forest protects the way, blocking others and changing their course to go around or head back towards where they came from. It's like a magical barrier.'

'So why am I here?' A sensation came over her that she already knew the answer.

'Because you are the last keeper of this world.'

She slid to the ground against one of the bookshelves and brought her knees to her chest. Hugging them she rocked back and forth. This information was so much to process. Only a few hours ago she had been crying like an infant she wasn't at the dance. It seemed so insignificant now compared to what she was being told. "So you, who are you?" It was easier for her to speak her thoughts out loud as if she were having an actual conversation with someone.

'We are the last guardians of this world. My name is Aslo and my wife is Kiera.'

"You have names. All this time you had names and didn't tell me. I thought I was crazy." A look of disbelief crossed over her pale face.

'Perhaps this is too much for you to take in all at once,' offered Kiera.

"No, I want to know everything. I want to know what happened to my parents," she barked.

'Alright,' Aslo responded. *'The other night you heard the basic story from Diana. Any extra details you need are contained in the books here which you can read any time. The world was divided by portals after the blood wars and guardians, keepers, portal guards and friends are the defence to keep all worlds safe. An ancient race found a way to contact men, who could be weakened and easily led. Another war broke out. Teams were sent to combat the threat. Your father was on one of the first teams.'*

'The threat was far more extensive than first believed. Weapons which could open up rifts in the space between worlds were being designed. An army had been growing behind our backs. More teams were sent to aid those already in battle. Soon our vulnerability was learnt. Although we guardians are immortal we can not travel the portals without a keeper and keepers are not immortal. Add on top of that only certain beings can be a keeper. The enemy figured out guardians could be trapped in worlds or specially made cages. They tricked keepers into worlds where guardians would be most useless and either killed or captured the keepers, leaving guardians stranded. Some were captured and confined in a world which we do not know the location of.'

"Couldn't another keeper just go through and bring back the guardians?" Willow asked.

'Yes, in theory, but each keeper could only carry two guardians. Keepers were low in numbers and it would have meant taking a big chance. At the time, losing more keepers wasn't in the plan especially since word had been sent all keepers were needed to join the fight.'

"How did they send word?" she interrupted the story again.

'Portal guards are telepathic. Each portal was to have two guards on each side. When a portal is open or active telepathic messages could flow through to the other side."Aslo paused for a moment then continued. "When a message was received here that help was needed, the remaining keepers had no choice but to answer. Your mother was one of them. She stayed with you as long as she could and then asked Kiera and myself to take care of you while she was gone. Less than a half a cycle after they left communication between the worlds stopped. Silence.'

Kiera picked up the story. 'Before the wars, there had been a prophecy of the destruction of this world and everything in it. The remaining council members took it to heart and decided the best thing they could do would be close the portals so no enemies could use them to travel here. All known portals were destroyed. We don't know who survived on the other side if anyone. The council later declared they were all dead. On that day things changed in this world.'

'No one knew that Aslo and I existed. We had not taken a keeper because I was pregnant, a rare occasion for our kind. The council removed all information they could find on guardians. We needed to take care of you and yet if someone saw us, it could put you in danger. Your parents were our friends. We decided to join with you, something that had never happened with a child under sixteen cycles. It worked, but we could only speak at first. Slowly we began to be able to move around and when the time came, I gave birth to eleven. Not only are you the only keeper under age but you carry thirteen guardians, when no one else could carry more than two. The downfall we can not separate from you until the exact day your sixteenth cycle begins.'

"My parents they could be alive? They were just left? Abandoned?" Tears were swelling in her eyes again.

Aslo answered. '*At the time the council was trying to protect those who were left and, in all fairness, there are thousands of different worlds, making chances of finding anyone slim if a rescue was attempted. The council changed after that from a role of teacher and mentor to ruler. They replaced the keeper spots with family members and removed everyone else outside the gates in hopes that memories would fade quickly, and they did. At the same time, the council forgot as well. They tasted power and, as in stories you have heard, their appetite grew. The same struggle we were fighting outside this world was taking over here as well. Their own self importance will be the downfall of this world if not from battle within, then as the prophecy foretold. If they had trained people how to use their powers to their fullest potential, perhaps you could have fought back. Most of you haven't even begun to discover the tip of what you can do.*'

"My dream...the attack...it will come from a hole in the sky, not the portals. That is what the dream meant isn't it?" Willow asked.

'*We believe so,*' Aslo added. '*We just don't know when. Only the council heard the original prophecy. We lived here and never mingled outside. That is why no one ever knew we existed. Only keepers had seen us before. The pregnancy was the first in thousands of cycles. We chose to stay put at the time.*'

"You risked their lives, your children, to join with me," Willow mumbled.

'*We loved you as our own. It was the only way. It was the right choice. All of us are fine and we were able to all be together. Pick a few books then walk to the left.*'

Willow picked a book about the main world and an encyclopedia of creatures the keepers had met in the different worlds, then moved to the left, there was a space between two book shelves. As she got closer, a staircase appeared winding downwards. She followed the stairs to a hallway.

"What is this place?" she asked.

'The keeper's living quarters. There are sitting rooms, weapons rooms, rooms to eat in and separate rooms to sleep in. Yours is five doors down on the right,' Aslo answered.

"Mine? But I'm not even old enough to be a keeper yet."

'You were always special. We always knew you would be a keeper, prophecies confirmed it as well and we always knew your abilities would be extra ordinary,' Kiera explained.

"I talk to trees and make it rain when I cry," she snorted.

'In time you will see child, it is so much more than that. We can help you develop those abilities you know you have but, you and only you, must discover what your abilities are for yourself. No one can tell you what you can or can not do.'

Her room was bigger than the shack she lived in. A large bed was in the centre of the floor, with a body cushion to lie on and warm blankets. On one side of the room there were cupboards and drawers filled with clothes, mainly black and all in her size. They were similar to the uniforms the guards wore and made of a material that could stretch but still protect.

"They were made for you try them on," Kiera said.

Willow was already changing. She pulled on black pants that were tight to her skin but still had incredible mobility and a black vest which was sleeveless and left areas of her back exposed. She became amused with the number of pockets the outfit had.

Out of the blue she asked, "Can I bring someone here who isn't a keeper?"

"If the need arises, yes," Aslo answered. "The boy, Nathan?"

"Yes, he could help me with all of the reading."

On the other side of the room was a desk with hair brushes and ties and a large mirror. She tied her hair back, jumped on the bed and began to read the book on the main world. Her mind swirled with images of tall buildings and metal objects that could move called cars.

The day had been so exciting and time had flown by. Willow drifted off to sleep with visions of the strange new world she had been reading about.

She opened her eyes and looked around. There was nothing...just plain white everywhere she looked. It took her a few minutes to figure out why she was there. "Of course, I am dreaming," she said smiling. "Ashlyn, can you hear me? Ashlyn?"

"I am here. Everyone is worried about you. Are you okay?"

Willow spun around and greeted her friend with a hug and a smile. "Yes, I am fine but I need you to do something for me. It's very important," she said. "I need you to ask Nathan to go to the forest and follow the path. Can you do that?"

"What path? To where?" Ashlyn face reflected confusion.

"Just ask him to trust me. When he gets to the forest he will find the path I am talking about. He has to come alone, it's very important. I will find him."

"Aren't you coming back?" her friend asked.

"Yes, soon, please don't tell anyone else about this either, just Nathan. We should go now," Willow said.

The room faded into the darkness of deep sleep.

Chapter Eight

The Sun was already shining when Willow walked back up the winding staircase and replaced the books to the spots from which she had borrowed them. As she walked around the semi-circular shelves, her fingers ran gently across the books that lined them as if taking in every title. Her attention then turned to the stone table. Walking over, she rounded it three times looking at all of its features. In each of the four corners was carved the same symbol that had been on the guards' arms. The corner pieces appeared to be separate from the table yet she couldn't move them. They all looked like smooth rocks, each with a flat top and the carving in the centre. Looking at the table again it seemed to her that the table had been built to match these rocks and not the other way round. She wondered if there might be a book that might explain it, but her thoughts were cut off.

"Willow, where are you?" Nathan's voice echoed on the wind.

She ran down the steps into the forest and the trees made way for a path which led right to the boy. Taking his hand, she led him back to the building where she had spent the night.

"What is this place?" he asked.

"Your Gran, her stories, they were all true. These books contain information on everything, on all the different worlds the guardians visited, maps, information on creatures and beings, locations of portals, encyclopedias of information and even languages. There is also information on us, records of abilities and instructions on how to train to maximize them."

His eyes widened in disbelief. "How do you know these books aren't just stories?" he asked.

She had to decide right then to trust him completely. She couldn't do this herself and if the end of their world was coming, she at least wanted to try to survive.

"A guardian told me," she answered. "I need your help, these books, I have to know what each one says, it's important. Things are changing and I think they are about to get a lot worse."

Nathan began his scanning of books and, at about the third, he looked at her curiously. "Red hair huh?"

"Sorry?"

"Red hair, according to this book means you have extreme abilities. It's very rare. In fact, it refers to the person as having powers which could make them a saviour of worlds. You must have pretty amazing talents. Do you know what they are yet?"

"I can talk to trees," she replied.

"Not sure how that can save a world but it's definitely interesting." He laughed a little. "Sorry," he added. This time they both broke out into laughter.

"I don't know either, I can make it rain when I cry too," she said after the two had settled down.

"That explains all the rain we have been having." He tried to not laugh but instead ended up letting out a snort starting the two giggling again.

"Let me see what you have read so far."

Nathan shared two books with her and over the next few hours he continued to read then share. In between, the two discussed some interesting points in one book or another. They talked about what the different shades of a pixie's wings meant, what a plane was and how big a world had to be to need to use one and how to find a dark elf that was cloaked in invisibility. Occasionally they spoke in different languages they had learnt from the books. They were at just over seventy of them and they hadn't even made a dent in the first shelf.

Willow went into the forest for a few minutes. "Kiera, Aslo are you there?" she asked.

'We are always here,' Kiera answered.

"Is there a room downstairs that isn't being used? One that Nathan could rest in if he gets tired?" she asked whispering.

'Yes the one past yours is empty, he could use that,' Aslo responded. *'Oh and you don't have to speak out loud we can still hear your thoughts.'*

"Right," she said still whispering. "I forgot for a moment."

She returned with a basket of fruit, which she set on the stone table.

Nathan eyes bulged, glistening at the sight of the fresh produce. "Thank goodness I was starting to wonder if I was ever going to see food again," he said taking a bit out of an apple.

"A little dramatic don't you think?" She said.

After eating she showed him how to find the staircase and his room if he was tired. Nathan's comments about being hungry had made her think about the others. It was time for her to go back and make sure they had food as well. After assuring him he would be safe and that she would be back as soon as possible, she headed to town.

Stepping into the forest she heard a playful whisper, "Ready to see what you can do?"

Willow smiled. Her eyes opened wide to take in what laid before her, a world she had only partially seen before. The tree in front of her swayed as if bowing and then branches formed a staircase for her to climb. She reached the top and peeked her head up above the tree line.

From beneath her she could hear a whispering, "Go ahead, we won't let you fall."

With that, she stepped on the branches and leaves and took her first steps across the top of the forest. It was beautiful the sun shining and wind tickling her face. She laid down, rolled around, taking in the different scents of each of the trees beneath her. Then she lay motionless on her back, her arms and legs outstretched, enjoying the feeling of the branches beneath her moving slowly in the wind, massaging her body gently. She closed her eyes. Visions of her friends entered her mind. Suddenly she realized time had been passing and she hadn't accomplished anything she had hoped to. Standing up she ran towards where the forest bordered town.

Chapter Nine

Jade decided to go into town earlier than the rest of her friends today. She was still ecstatic about how well the dance had gone the night before. Even the short downpour couldn't ruin her victory. But she had one last conquest to make. She would have what she wanted and show that town of ingrates their place, beneath her.

She had a skip to her walk as she came down the lane, carrying a closed basket on her arm and completely oblivious to anything going on around her. Most of the town's population was standing in the middle of the road. She smiled as she passed them, stopping at Mr. and Mrs. Shinning with Victoria in tow.

"Good morning, are your boys up?" she asked, not even noticing the solemn looks on their faces.

"They are inside," Opaque answered without looking at her.

She thanked them and continued on to their house. Opening the door, her eyes fixed on a glass case elegantly displaying the jewelry that had been made for Willow to wear to the dance. A devious smile crossed her face as she walked by and called out for the brothers. Pete answered her, extending his hand to offer her a seat in the visiting room behind the shop area.

"Where are your brothers?" she asked. "I brought you some more cake."

Pete's eyes widened at the thought of the food she was offering. He had never liked sweets very much, but this was like nothing he had tasted before. Just the thought of it made his mouth water and his heart race. His adrenaline was pumping, he needed to have it, needed it now, more than anything in the world.

He yelled for his brothers loudly, letting them know Jade had brought more of the cake. His mouth filled with saliva as he watched her bring the baked delicacy out from the basket that adorned her arm. The other two boys were there in a flash, both experiencing the same reaction as their brother.

Jade served them each a piece, watching carefully as they quickly devoured it. As she filled their plates again, finishing the rest of the cake, she mentioned that there were some things that would make her happy, very happy. The boys, still consumed by the food before them, didn't answered her. A look of aggravation crossed her face which she quickly changed back to a pleasant smile as she pulled out a second cake from her basket.

"I thought you boys might be extra hungry today, we were out so late and all," she said watching the boy's eyes following the cake as she set it on the table.

When the boys had almost finished the cake, Jade spoke again. "You fellas happy?" she asked.

The three brothers' attention switched to the girl in front of them. They nodded longing for more words to sing to them. Jade wouldn't disappoint them.

"I wish I could be happy. Until this sadness is banished from my life, I can not give an answer as to who I will chose to live out the rest of my life with. I want to, but I just can't think of such joy," she said her face filling with sadness.

"What can I do to make you feel the same joy your presence gives me?" Jessie asked kneeling before her. "Name the task, there is nothing I wouldn't do to see your beautiful face smile again."

Turning her head and faking tears, she replied speaking to them all, "Perhaps." She paused for a moment letting the brothers hang on her word anticipating more. "The dress and jewelry that were made for Willow for the dance, I cried for days when I learnt such beauty would be worn by someone else. If I could just wear them and feel worthy of such items." She sighed.

That was enough for the boys who rushed out to the front shop. Jessie and Dezi began fighting each other, tugging the jewelry case back and forth, while Pete slipped out the door and headed to the seamstress's shop. He found the black dress lying on the counter. Picking it up he rushed back. Not even noticing the state of his parents' shop, filled with broken glass and destroyed furniture, or his brothers still battling, he slipped past to Jade with her prize.

Jade held up the dress and smiled. Folding it neatly, she packed it safely away in her basket. The two other boys emerged, bruised and cut, each carrying items she longed for. Dezi presented her with the necklace and earrings, while Jessie had the hair piece.

"For me?" She squealed with delight putting the pieces into her basket and closing the lid. "This is so much to process, you all have made me so happy. I have to think about my choices, but I will have an answer for you tomorrow. Until then dream of our time together."

The boys sat back with silly lovestruck smiles on their faces as they watched Jade leave.

Jade had a quick skip to her step, smiling ear to ear. She stopped to pick up food for the day, when she realized the stands were empty. Turning around she saw the whole town standing behind her. She walked closer and asked, "Where is the vegetable girl?"

"We don't know," Clairity answered. "She has been gone since last night."

"I see," Jade replied with a shrug, continuing her walk to the castle without a thought or care.

Most of the council were gathered at a table in the dining room deciding who would go into town today for supplies when Jade walked in.

"Where have you been so early today?" her mother asked.

"I went to town to thank the boys for such a wonderful evening," she said still beaming from the prizes hidden in her basket.

"You should have brought back some fruit," her father said without looking at her.

"I tried, but couldn't. The useless girl ran away or something," she responded with a couldn't care less tone.

"What have you done?" Nebulah demanded.

"What have I done?" Anger Spiked in Jade's voice. " What have I done? I can't help it if I am more beautiful than her. How is that my fault. I am sure she just went off to pout her date decided he wanted to be with me more than her."

"Didn't you have enough dates last night without one more? Couldn't you let that girl have a little bit of happiness? Did I bring you up to feel nothing?" Her mother waved one hand in front of her face, her mouth slightly open. She looked upwards attempting to stop tears from falling.

"You brought me up to see that we are far better than those losers. That we deserve to be treated better and have everything we want. None of them deserve to make me or anyone else from the castle feel inferior and in no way should those people show us up or make fools of us and, let's face it, lately that's all they have been doing while you sit here and do nothing. They need to be put in their place. All I did is what this council hasn't had the nerve to do," Jade said a green fire burning in her eyes.

"How dare you pretend you know the business of this council and try to hide your deeds behind it's name." Malarchy stood, fury written on his face. "You will go to your room and remain there until a proper punishment has been decided on. Do not test me further child."

Jade let out a little scream and left for her room.

Malarchy stood silent for a few moments staring at the still blank wall before speaking. "Nyssa, Zebulon, Nebulah, would you please take a few guards into town? See if you can find out what happened, assess the damage and see if the guards can harvest any food from Willow's gardens. Although I fear not."

"Why wouldn't they be able to pick our food for us?" Aurora asked.

Malarchy chuckled. "Do you really think that much food grows naturally every day? That fruit trees have new fruit every day? No, I am afraid it was the girl who made it happen. That is why I let her remain on her own and not join the orphanage years ago. Without her, we could all starve."

"There is still the bakery, Malarchy," Aurora added.

This time he laughed. "The bakery, yes well out back of the bakery is a plot of land where the grains grow that the bakery uses to make its food. Who do you think makes them grow everyday? And then there is the matter of the weather."

"The weather?" Nyssa asked as if surprised.

"Yes the weather," he answered. "Since the day that child was born we have enjoyed bright skies, warm temperatures, only adequate rainfall and at the same time everyday, while we sleep so it disturbs nothing. The sun sets and rises at the same time."

"Are you saying she controls the weather as well and did so as a baby?" Nyssa asked.

"That is exactly what I am saying. She is a terra former, a rare ability, not to mention it has been with her since her birth. Something we have never seen before. No, I am afraid if we can't somehow fix this mess, things will get bad. The sooner you get going, the faster we can try to resolve this. The rest of us will work on alternate plans taking the worst scenario into mind."

When Nebulah, Zebulon, Nyssa and the four guards reached the city, they found the town still congregated in the street. They approached the gathering, sending everyone back to their homes, while the guards looked at the gardens. Some of the townsfolk had moved to their porches but were still watching as the guards returned with bad news. There was nothing growing...nothing at all. Not even a fruit tree, just plain open space.

A chilling scream came from the Shinning house. The council members hurried to the door and let themselves in. At first glance one might have thought the sight of their front shop was enough to let out such a screech of terror as had just been heard. Glass lined the floor, all of the display cases were destroyed, there was damage to the walls and windows, but after carefully stepping through the mess they saw the Shinnings kneeling over their three sons on the floor. The boys were all having some sort of seizure, unconscious with a froth coming from their mouths.

"Send for Micca!" Nebulah yelled to the guards behind her. "And quickly there is no time to waste. Your fastest must go."

"Help is on its way," Nyssa said to Augusto. "Can you tell us what happened?"

"I don't know. We were outside with the others. The only one who came by was Jade," he answered.

Opaque stood picked up the broken case which had held Willow's jewelry, looked at the bits of cake left on the table, then turned to Nebulah. "Your daughter did this," she said

"I don't think now is the time for accusations."

"The things we made for Willow for the dance are gone...stolen. She threatened she would have them no matter what the cost." Opaque picked up a plate and took it to Jade's mother. "This cake...she brought it here this morning."

No one had noticed Martha was standing in the background until she added, "The dress I made Willow is gone as well."

"Stay here," Nebulah said to Nyssa and Zebulon. "I will take a guard and return to the castle. If my daughter is involved I will find out."

Leaving, she almost bumped into Willow, who had come over to see what all the commotion was about.

Willow looked inside and saw the three boys on the floor. "What's wrong with them," she shrieked. "Victoria, she could help, she can heal."

She felt a hand fall on her shoulder and turned to see Micca behind her. He pushed past and knelt over the boys.

"She can't help," Micca said. "It's not anything a healer can cure. They have consumed a potion of some sort. The only way to save them now is to find out what the ingredients were and make a counter potion."

"Who would do this? Why?" Willow asked.

Augusto answered. "We think it was Jade."

"Is this over me? Did she do this because of me?" Her eyes stung.

Zebulon put his arm around her. "Come now child, you need some air. Let's not have tears and flood the town. We will figure this out. How about you tend to some food for the rest of the townsfolk. There are hungry, scared people."

Willow looked at him with a blank stare and stepped outside. He knew what she could do. What she didn't understand was why the people didn't just go harvest there own food. She stumbled across the road, still in shock from the sight of the boys and round to her garden. It was empty, she stood dumfounded, there was nothing.

Clairity and Ashlyn had come to her side. They both were just as shocked by the sight of the empty fields, but what came next was even more unusual.

Willow stood tall raising her arms and what looked like a golden dust rained down on the field. With in seconds there were bountiful fruit trees, bushes of berries, vines with grapes and vegetables of all types fully grown and ready to pick. She turned and stepped towards her friends, but the weight of the day's events became too much for her and her legs buckled, sending her tumbling to the ground.

Chapter Ten

Nebulah walked right by the other council members and into the castle. She was keeping a fast pace which didn't slow once inside. She climbed the staircase and went right to Jade's room. Flinging her daughter's door open, she moved straight to the bed.

"What are these?" she demanded pointing to the missing items from town.

"Can't knock?" Jade snarled back at her.

"What is going on here?" Malarchy having seen his wife return, followed her. He was standing at the door looking in.

Nebulah turned to him. "These items were stolen from town today," she said choking back tears.

"They were gifts, daddy, from the Shinning brothers. Go ask them," she said giving her mother a look of disgust.

"He can't ask them, they are unconscious and having seizures, all three. The only one to see them today was you Jade," Nebulah replied. "What did you do?"

"Don't be so dramatic mother. I am sure they will be fine tomorrow," Jade said without concern.

"If something happens to those boys and you have information that can save them." Her mother's words cut off as she grabbed the dress and gems off her daughter's bed.

"Hey, those are mine what do you think you are doing?" Jade yelled.

"Returning them to their owners," Nebulah replied. She was about to leave when Nyssa appeared behind Malarchy.

"I am afraid there is bad news. The boys ingested some form of a potion, without an ingredients list, they won't make it," Nyssa said as she passed Malarchy in the doorway and looked at the items Nebulah was holding. All three turned their attention to the girl.

"Why are you looking at me?" Jade demanded. "Fine, it wasn't poison. It was just a little love potion and I didn't make it." She looked straight at Nyssa and added, "If you want to know what was in it, why don't you ask Camile. Their fate is her fault, not mine."

"You have broken so many rules..."

Jade interrupted her father with a cold voice. "So change them. That's what the council does isn't it? Makes things fit the way they want them to?"

"You have no idea what you have done. I am not sure we can help you out of this mess." Her father had a sadness in his voice, something Jade hadn't heard before.

"I can't believe you are my daughter," her mother sobbed.

"I wish you were dead," Jade yelled back at her in a fit of anger.

The three council members left the room and locked the door behind them. They found Camile in the front sitting room. News of the situation in town had already spread through out the castle.

"I'm sorry," the girl blurted out in tears. "I didn't mean to. I told Jade not to use so much. She went crazy over that girl getting invited to the dance, said she need to teach her a lesson or all our futures would be ruined. She said our parents would be proud. I don't know why I believed her. I didn't think she would hurt anyone, honest."

"Later," her mother said with a hand on each of Camile's shoulders. "Right now we need to go to town and tell Micca everything you did to make that potion."

Nebulah told her husband she would join the two heading into town and return the missing items. Before leaving she faced her husband. "Are we being punished for what we have done?" she asked.

Malarchy answered, "I think so. This is my fault I have been so blind. Do what you can in town. Jade is locked in her room. There will have to be a hearing and she will have to answer for her actions."

*****

Jade looked around her room. She was less than impressed that she had been locked in her room and even worse that her mother had taken the items she had worked so hard to get. Why didn't they see what she did was for everyone? The Council was getting soft, losing control, letting inferiors have their way and running to their aid. Her anger spiked at the thought of her own parents taking the sides of those nobodies over her.

With nothing to do, she laid down on her bed and hugged her favourite doll. Closing her eyes, she was somewhere between the state of sleep and wake when she heard a voice call her name. Opening her eyes she was somehow in a white room with a man standing in front of her.

"Where am I?" she asked.

"In a dream," he replied. "My family can all dream walk. We unlocked the secrets to that ability long ago. But that is not important now, what is important is you. I heard your cries, my dear. What has happened to you is unjust. A beautiful talented woman like yourself should be bowed down to, treated as a queen, not locked up like a common criminal. The people around you don't understand your brilliance like I do."

"You do?" she asked.

He moved next to her and brushed her face gently. "Yes, I have been watching you in your dreams for some time. I have seen your thoughts and desires...your plans and aspirations. You are exactly what I have looked for to stand beside me, to be adored by all as I adore you."

"Who are you?" she asked.

"Forgive me, I am Prince Joseph, son of King Cornelius, saviour of worlds, at your service," he answered now standing in front of her.

He was beautiful, with short platinum blonde hair, cold blue eyes and stunning features. His body looked chiseled to perfection like a statue, with just enough muscles in all the right places. She couldn't help but feel they would make the perfect couple and have beautiful children.

Knowing her thoughts he smiled. "Yes, together we could rule worlds. I would give you only the finest jewels and clothes. Others could only hope to be you. Everything your heart desires I could hand you on a golden platter. I will make anything you have wished for come true."

"Please, I want to go with you," she answered without thought.

"And I want nothing more than to take you my darling, but I need your help, to enter your world so we can leave together and live the life you deserve," he answered.

"What can I do? Tell me," she pleaded.

"Is there someone in your world who can mutate or bend objects like metal?" he asked.

"Yes of course, Neil can."

"Good, I need you to convince him to stretch the sky," he said.

"I don't understand," she answered.

"Yes, of course. When he bends metal he is actually changing the molecular density of the item for a short period of time. If he concentrates hard enough on the sky he can weaken the boundaries between our worlds for a short time allowing me to open a way in and out for just long enough to come for you," he explained.

"How do I convince him to do this?" she asked.

"You are a beautiful woman. Convince him you know a way to run away with him. Tell him you two will be together forever if he helps you escape the wrath of the council. We both know their punishment will be severe."

"Okay, how will you know when it is done?" she asked.

"I will watch the skies my queen. Do not doubt, when it is done I will come and you will have everything you have ever wished for. Oh and one last thing, should the council wish to impose a punishment on you, they don't have the right. Tell them that only Acacia can decide your fate. It is your right." He kissed her cheek gently and faded away into the distance.

*****

By the time Nebulah, Nyssa and Camile arrived back at the Shinning house, the guards had cleaned up all the broken glass and debris in the shop and removed all furniture from the sitting area. The room was now bare with only the three boys lying on the floor and Micca hovering over them trying to do what he could. The way his long black hair was neatly tied back in a pony tail, so it wouldn't get in the way, showed off the other features of his face. His high eyebrows and intense brown eyes, together with the stubble beginnings of a beard made him look almost attractive in a rough manly sort of way. He noticed the new visitors and moved towards them.

"Do we have any information?" he asked anxiously.

"Camile can tell you what was used," Nyssa offered.

Nebulah motioned she would be back and headed over to Martha's to return the dress and jewels. She had hoped to avoid the boys' parents for the moment until their sons had been cured of the condition her daughter had caused.

Camile stepped forward. "It was a love potion. Jade wanted the boys to ask her to the dance instead of any of them taking Willow." She took a piece of paper out of her pocket and handed it to Micca. "I told her not to give them too much. I warned her things could go wrong. I would never hurt anyone."

Micca read over this list and let out a breath of air loudly. "This is an advanced potion, the items in it are hard to obtain. I don't even know how you came about this recipe. We could search the forest for days and never find the plants and roots we need to create an antidote and to be honest, we don't have that much time."

"Willow!" Nyssa exclaimed. "Is she still in town?"

"Yes, she is resting at her friend's house, Clairity. But how will that help us?" he asked.

"She can grow anything. It's part of her abilities. She could grow the plants you need right here in seconds," Nyssa said.

"If she can do that, we could save these boys. Could someone bring her here? Time is running out."

Two guards woke willow from her sleep and summoned her to Micca. They filled her in on the details of what had transpired on the way.

"What do you need?" she asked upon arriving, skipping all pleasantries.

The next hour the two spent outside. Micca would describe a plant and Willow would grow any that resembled its description. He could then pick the one he needed and harvest the flower, leaf or root required for the potion. After that came the juicing, cutting, blending of ingredients and a touch of magic. Once finished the antidote was administered to all three boys and all there was to do was wait.

Nebulah was waiting in the background, not wanting to disturb the process but anxious for information as to the outcome.

"Will they be okay?" she finally asked getting the attention of everyone else waiting.

"We won't know for a bit yet, the antidote needs a chance to run through their bodies. It should work, if the list I was given was complete. It is close though, the poison has been in them a long time," Micca answered.

"And Jade?" Willow asked without looking at Nebulah.

"She will be treated as anyone would who committed such an act. Punishment will be severe I am sure and the town will be invited to the hearing if they wish to attend," Nebulah answered without emotion. "The afternoon of the second sunrise from now should give sufficient time for the fate of the boys to be known and a trial before council to be readied." She turned and left the house, heading back to the castle to give the news to her husband. Camile and Nyssa followed behind her not knowing what to say but understanding Camile too would have to answer for her part in the deception.

Willow walked outside and sat on the front steps. Clairity had been waiting outside and promptly sat down beside her. There were still a few hours of daylight left. The town was quiet and empty.

"It isn't over yet," Clairity said breaking the silence. "Something is coming. I can feel it."

"No, it isn't over," Willow replied to her friend. "Everything is happening so fast I don't know if I can keep up. I don't know if I want to. Three weeks ago life was so much easier. Ignorance is bliss."

"What do you think they will do to her?" Clairity asked.

"Not sure, I guess it depends on whether or not." Her words stopped. It was the first time she realized her friends could actually die. A lump grew in her throat and tears began to swell in her eyes. At the same time, clouds appeared in the sky and bits of rain scattered began to fall. She took a deep breath and said, "stop," out loud. The clouds swirled and vanished from sight.

Her friend was in awe. "You did that!" she exclaimed not as a question but rather a statement. "I totally saw you make those clouds come and go."

Willow would have normally been happy to share every detail she had learnt about her abilities in the last day, but now wasn't the time. She couldn't be enthusiastic about anything with Jessie, Dezi and Pete fighting for their lives. She nodded to her friend affirming that the weather change was her doing.

The girls heard the door close behind them and spun their heads round to see Micca. He sat down beside Willow.

"They seem to be responding well so far. The seizures have stopped and colour is returning to their bodies. It was lucky you were here. That's some talent you have," he said.

"How long before they wake up? I'd like to be here, but I have to be back to the forest for dark. I have some research I am doing with a friend. It's important."

"Research? That sounds interesting. What exactly are you researching?" he asked back.

Willow had to think quick. She wasn't ready to let everyone know about the Kiera and Aslo, not until they could officially separate from her anyway. She also couldn't say prophecies about the end of the world and probably not a good idea to say she was trying to figure out how to find out if her parents were still alive. "How to talk to trees," she blurted out. Seeing the strange looks she was getting from both sides of her she added, "I think we have discovered that they react differently to common words. It's fascinating really."

Micca chuckled. "I bet it is. If all goes as planned the boys should be moving about anytime, so you should get back to your tree conversations on time." He stood up and went back inside the house.

After the door had closed, Clairity turned to her and said, "How to talk to trees? Really? You are so bad at lying."

"Come with me tonight and I can show you." She hoped her friend would catch on to her reluctance to discuss things in front of listening ears.

"Not much else to do around here at the moment. I'll ask mom."

Only a few moments after Clairity left, the door behind them opened and Jessie stumbled out still shaky on his legs. He sat down on the steps and rubbed his neck.

"How are you feeling?" Willow asked.

"Like I almost died. Stiff and aching everywhere, every muscle and joint," he answered.

"Your brothers?"

"Fine, just taking a bit longer to walk about. It would be nice if someone would tell us what happened."

"You don't know?"

"No, last thing I remember I was talking with Dezi and Pete about the dance. I was thinking I would ask Ashlyn and Pete would ask Clairity so we could all go together."

"Would have been nice," Willow said looking down.

"Did something happen to one of the girls?" he asked with a look of concern.

"No, no. But the dance was last night. You went with Jade. All three of you."

Micca had stepped outside just in time to hear the what she said. "Perhaps Jessie should take some time before getting into the details of what happened. I don't want too much information too fast to cause shock."

"Sorry. I didn't know," Willow replied.

"I want to know," Jessie said holding his head.

"Later, your parents can fill you in with the details. For now you need rest. Back inside."

After saying their goodbyes, Willow walked up the street to the Posh house. Clairity and her mother were standing outside and she filled them in with the condition of the brothers. Her friend had a bag with some clothes and personal items ready.

"Where will you girls stay?" Mrs. Posh asked.

"A fort," Willow answered. "In the forest, it's well hidden and safe."

"Sounds exciting. You girls be safe and if anything happens, anything at all, come right back. You understand? Both of you?"

The girls nodded and headed off together into the forest. Once out of sight Willow asked her friend, "Do you trust me?" Without waiting for an answer, she grabbed Clairity's hand and climbed a staircase of branches to the top of the trees. Her friend was speechless and excited. Together the girls walked on top of the forest all the way back to where Nathan was waiting. Following a staircase down, Clairity was stunned by the sight of the stone building standing before her. Before she could speak, Willow grabbed her hand, moved inside and explained the story with Nathan's help.

The three spent the evening learning from Nathan about the books he had read and talking about far off exotic lands. The two girls would later spend the night in Willow's room together, Nathan sleeping soundly in the bedroom beside them.

The next morning after they had fruit for breakfast. Nathan found a book specifically outlining how to train a seer to develop visions more clearly. Clairity and Nathan decided to spend the day trying to expand her psychic abilities, while Willow went into town to grow food for the people and check on the condition of Jessie, Dezi and Pete. She returned in the afternoon with not much to report. The boys were stronger but still lacked memories of what happened and the hearing for Jade was still scheduled for the next day, which Willow planned to attend.

Chapter Eleven

Sabrina and Justin walked into the castle's sitting room and sat down to join Neil. The scandalous events of the last few weeks were on the tips of their tongues. The news had spread quickly of Jade's and Camile's confinement to quarters pending the outcome of tomorrow's hearing.

"If you are here to discuss Jade, I don't want to hear it. She is still my friend and she isn't here to tell us what happened," Neil said not wasting time.

"Poor Camile is locked up because of her, or did you forget she is our friend too," Sabrina replied.

"How do you know it wasn't Camile's idea?" he asked.

Everyone was sure Sabrina had known about the love potion and perhaps was even in on the plans, but she wasn't about to confess to anything and end up in a hearing herself.

"I just believe Camile. That's all," she responded. "If you want Jade's version, why don't you go talk to her? Let's face it, we all know the reason you are taking her side is because you have a crush on her. Perhaps you don't want to believe she gave a love potion to three other guys?"

"Even if she did give a love potion to that lot, it wasn't because she was interested in any of them. I guarantee that."

Neil didn't want to continue the argument any further than it had gone, especially since his name might also come up at the hearing tomorrow as a supporter if he wasn't careful. But thinking about what Sabrina had said, she was right. He needed to go talk to Jade and to hear her side of the story for himself.

He climbed the staircase and came to the door to her room. There was a magic lock on the door which could not be opened by anyone other than Ozias. He slid the palm of his hand on the smooth wood and after getting up enough courage, he knocked.

"Jade, are you there?"

Jade moved to the door on the other side and put her ear against it. "Neil? Is that you?"

"Yes," he said with a smile. "I wanted to check on you, make sure you were okay, well as best as you could be."

Both slid to the floor and sat in front of their sides of the door.

"Yeah, I guess...It isn't how people are making it out. It didn't happen that way. You believe me don't you?" she asked.

"I figured that. Camile is having her hearing after yours so hopefully she will admit to what she did."

"Camile is having a hearing? I figured it was just me." She had a touch of remorse in her voice. "I don't want to let her life be ruined too. The Council is going to come down hard on me, make and example of me. I know that."

"There must be something we can do."

"Well...there is one chance, but it's risky and I would need your help." Jade carefully listened for the tone of Neil's voice. It would tell her if she had a chance or not.

After a few minutes he responded, "What would I have to do?"

Jade smiled, "You know how you do those tricks, changing the way a rock looks and bending metal without touching it?"

"Sure." He loved making things look strange and getting a reaction when people saw it.

"If you could do that...with the sky."

"What?" he answered.

"Hear me out," she pleaded. "If you concentrated on doing that to the sky, it would weaken the boundaries between worlds and create an opening, for a short period of time, just long enough for us to escape together to another world and start a brand new life together."

"How do you know this?"

"I...found a book in one of the restricted rooms dad forgot to lock once. It outlined the whole procedure. Seems easy enough and it's not permanent so no one would get hurt and I would be free. If I don't, I won't see you or anyone else again for many cycles."

"You don't know that Jade. Your parents."

"My parents," she laughed, "are the ones looking for the most sever sentence. They are going to use me to show the town they have the people's interests in mind. To stop any possible fall out, uprising or riots. They don't need me, they have my brother. He has been their favourite since he was born. No my parents aren't going to lift a finger to help me. They already sealed my fate."

"I don't know Jade. We don't even know what's out there. We could walk right into something horrible."

"How horrible could it be? We would be together, forever," Jade replied.

"Someone is coming I have to go. I will see you tomorrow. Don't worry I will figure something out."

Neil stood up and walked towards the stairs just as two guards turned the corner. He motioned a hello to them and headed downstairs. He definitely had a lot to think about.

Chapter Twelve

Clairity and Nathan chose to remain in the forest reading books for the day, so Willow met Ashlyn and they headed to the castle together, arriving shortly before the hearing was to take place. All of the adults from town had already assembled to hear the council's sentence for the crimes that had been committed. Jade was sitting on one side of the council's table and Camile was seated on the other, presumably to keep the two from talking and perhaps fabricating a story about the events that had happened the past few weeks. Jessie, Dezi and Pete were not asked to the hearing, mainly because they still had no recollection of anything that transpired, so they stayed at home with Victoria.

The council were in their best dress and had already taken their spots. Some of the younger children of the castle were also in attendance. Jade's brother, Jordan, who had only just reached his sixth cycle, ran up and hugged his sister. A chorus of '*awe*' rang out from the crowd. Jordan was adorable. He was the sort of kid you see and can't help but pay attention to, his personality demanded it. From his short mushroom top hair cut, to the dimples when he smiled, he reeked of cuteness and no matter what he did someone always found him entertaining and delightful.

Nebulah left her spot at the council table and led her son away from his sister choosing to have him sit with her so as not to interrupt anything important once they got started.

Zebulon led the hearing, calling for silence and then explaining how the proceeding would be held. The first part would be fact taking from witnesses, followed by questioning the two girls, deliberation of the council and then results and punishments, if any.

Most of the morning was spent calling witnesses. There was Augusto and Opaque, Martha and Olie, Micca, all of the guards who had gone to town over the past few days, and various others from town who saw the basket or heard the threats against Willow and her friends.

After a short break for lunch, Zebulon began the questioning of Jade.

"Did you use an unauthorized love potion on Jessie, Dezi and Pete Shinning?" he asked.

"Yes," Jade answered without hesitation.

"When did you decide to do this?"

"When I saw the things people were making for Vegetable...Willow. There was something special about them, not like items made for me. I felt inferior and angry, so I made a plan." She twiddled her thumbs waiting for the next question.

"Who did you tell your plan to?" Zebulon asked.

Jade decided right then she knew she was going down but Camile didn't have to. She felt sorry for involving her friend and being less than honest with her. Perhaps telling the truth might get her some leniency. "No one," she answered.

The crowd buzzed with talk after hearing that answer and Zebulon called for silence. "Who made the potion?" he asked.

"Camile, but she didn't know my plan," Jade replied her voice shaky.

"But she did make the potion?"

"Yes, but please, let me tell you what happened," she pleaded.

"Very well," Zebulon replied. "I will allow this. Please continue."

"I was upset after returning home for the second time and still being told I couldn't have the beautiful things made for someone else. I was outraged they said no to my mother as well. There is a place I go to when I am upset, down stairs an old sitting room, but this time a door had been left open to a restricted room, I went inside. It looked as if it used to be a library. I peaked through some of the books and found one on potions."

"I was hoping to give Willow a few warts or something on the day of the dance, but I found the love potion. I ripped it out of the book, thinking I could steal her date and end up with the things that were made for her. No one would ever know. The recipe said that the recipient wouldn't remember once it wore off. Eager, I asked Camile to make it for me. I told her it was a prank I was playing on Willow, no other details. I made it impossible for her to say no. I had her make extra just in case it wore off earlier than expected. She warned me not to give anyone too much or something bad could happen. I didn't listen. I gave the boys the cake. I alone deserve punishment."

"That is very honest of you. Why would you offer up such honesty now when we have already heard you incriminated Camile as responsible?" Zebulon queried.

"I have had time to think, sitting alone. I don't want to ruin Camile's life when she did nothing wrong," Jade answered.

"But she did do something wrong. She made the love potion for you."

"Because I made her and I convinced her our parents would be proud," Jade cried out.

"Very well. The council shall review this information and be back with the decision." Zebulon said leaving the makeshift court.

Jade looked through the crowd and her eyes rested on Neil. She wondered what he was thinking right now...if he knew how she had tried to trick him into making a passage for her to be with her new found love.

Jordan came back and hugged her again. As much as she had disliked him and the attention he stole from her, he still loved his sister. She looked into his eyes and hugged him back for the first time.

The council returned quickly. Nebulah took Jordan's hand again this time she had a tear in her eye and they remained close. Malarchy stood on the other side of his daughter. The crowd was loud with anticipation of what was about to be revealed. Zebulon stood and again called for silence.

"Jade, it has been decided that you did cause harm to another, wilfully or not, by use of an illegal substance, for personal gain. The council has decided that you shall be kept under lock in the guard house, without visitation rights for five cycles and during such time you shall be delegated work to be done to aid the orphanage."

Jade's knees went weak. This was far worse than she had anticipated. She remembered the words she had been told in her dream and blurted out, "You have no authority to cast such a sentence only Acacia can pass judgement by law."

Malarchy's face went white and he screamed, "Noooooo." It was too late the earth rumbled and quaked as a great tree rose up on the hill. "Foolish girl, now your life is forfeit."

Ashlyn turned to Willow. "It's now, it's happening now," and ran off in the direction of the hill.

Everything was moving so fast, people were scared. Neil took a few steps backwards and almost tripped over Willow. He was staring at Jade saying *'No'* over and over. Then all of a sudden he looked at the sky and raised his hands. For a moment it looked as if the sky was a rubber ball, bouncing up and down. People were running, Malarchy was holding Jade and Nebulah was holding Jordan beside them.

Suddenly the sky ripped open. An army of men instantly appeared, dressed in red and black. Willow noticed Neil wasn't moving. She grabbed his arm pulling him behind her, they ran. Camile caught up to them when they stopped at the gates. Willow grabbed Faramund's arm pleading him to tell her where Diana was being kept.

"In the guard house," he answered. "I will make sure she gets out safely."

Willow nodded. "Head with Diana into the forest. It's the only place with cover from the enemy. I will find you and lead you to shelter." She disappeared with Neil and Camile into trees heading to the only place she knew they couldn't be found.

Chapter Thirteen

"Well boys looks like we hit the jackpot!" Joseph said to his brothers as they walked through the newly formed hole in the fabric between worlds, an army of men following behind. "Our sisters will be buying dinner tonight."

"How do you want to split it up?" Lance asked.

"You and Simon head to town, empty it, then move into that forest area. Split it up how you want. My team will take the castle and castle grounds. How much time do we have?"

"Just over two hours," Simon replied.

"Men, we have about two hours no fooling around. Let's get to work," Joseph yelled.

It took only moments for Joseph and his men to reach the stone table. "Secure that lot," he ordered motioning to Jade and her family. He stepped up on the table. "And the rest at the table here. Put them in one group beside the princess. Leave a few men to help keep them here." He turned his attention to the others in the grounds. "Ladies and gentlemen," he yelled. "If I could have your attention. If you run or give my men any issues they will kill you. I suggest you stay put and wait to be processed as a prisoner of war."

He jumped down with a smile. "This is fun isn't it?" he said brushing Jade's hair with his hand. "And I want to thank you for your role darling."

"This wasn't what we agreed to," Jade said shaking.

"Ah now, now, we never actually discussed what would happen to your world. Did you think you could have all those things you want without people to serve? Worlds to rule are conquered worlds my dear. Maybe you should have asked more questions before you were willing to sell your soul? Ah, but don't worry. I am a man of my word and you shall have everything you have ever wished for."

He turned to one of his men. "Take the brother."

"Noooo. Jordan. No. You can't. What are you doing?" she cried.

"You wished he would go away and you would be an only child. I am making that happen for you," he smirked as he watched his man drag the crying child away.

"That's not what I wanted," she shrieked.

"Perhaps not, but it is what you wished." Joseph rounded the group gathered before him tapping on their shoulders. He enjoyed the pain he was causing her. It was his game. His amusement for the day.

He stopped behind her mother, looked straight into Jade's eyes and snapped her neck. Nebulah's body fell to the ground lifeless.

"NOOOOOOOOOOOOOOOOOOOOOO!" Jade cried in hysterics.

"You wished many times she was dead."

"I didn't mean it. I...was angry. I would never. I take it back. I...take it back. Please!" she pleaded.

"It doesn't work that way I am afraid. Death even I can't undo. Lesson learned...careful what you wish for, it might come true," he said still walking.

"I wish you would leave us alone," Jade said. Her father was hugging her now, trying to keep his eyes off the lifeless body of his wife.

"Interesting," he said treating her statement as a twist to his game. He had taken out a dagger and was tapping the blade on his lips. "I was going to enjoy you this evening. I suppose another one of these young girls will do. Very well, as you wish."

He motioned to a man who came running awaiting orders. "Take these two to the town and leave them there. They are not to be harmed." He turned to Jade. "You and your father will be alone as you wish. The only people left in this world when the necrid flames engulf all you know and burn the flesh of your body while you feel every second." He sat cross legged on the stone table laughing as he indicated to the other men to bring the remainder of the group for processing. Then he began whistling a song while watching his victory unfold.

Chapter Fourteen

It didn't take long for Willow to move Camile and Neil through the forest. They were almost at the hidden quarters when they stumbled upon Jessie, Dezi and Pete, with Arnold following behind them.

"Follow me," she said. "I know the only safe place we can go." There was no time to explain. She needed to keep moving, the invaders were close behind. Words of caution whispered on the leaves of the trees providing her with news of others hiding in the forest. All she could do was find as many people as she could before the invaders did.

The group arrived at the building and were greeted by Clairity and Nathan. Both were worried, sensing something was wrong and seeing the state of those who were arriving. Willow had forgotten they knew nothing of what had happened.

"They can fill you in later," Willow said catching her breath. "I need to get back out there and look for others who may have survived."

"Survived?" Clairity shrieked.

"Yes, listen to me everyone, this is the safest place you can be. No one can find you here, but you have to stay inside. If you stray to the forest, you will not find your way back. Clairity, Nathan, explain to them when I am gone."

The two nodded they would and Willow turned to leave adding once again, "No matter what you hear or think you see, no one can find you. You must trust me." She disappeared into the trees.

The group went about trying to fill each other in as best they could with the information they had. Fear made a thickness in the air choking them of their sensibility. The situation became worse when the voices of men talking about tracking people became clear. They were close.

"This is crazy," Arnold said. "We are waiting to be picked off one by one. This is not even a proper building. When they find us, they have an open shot. I'm not waiting to die in this death trap. We found this place, they will too." He ran for the forest before anyone could stop him.

He had only gotten a few steps when he first turned around to see if any of the others were following him. He stopped dead in his tracks, the building, the others, everything was gone. He tried to back track but ended up running into a group of the invaders with cross bows.

"Stop there!" a man yelled.

Arnold ran.

"Bring him down," another voice said. Almost instantly an arrow flew through the air and with exact precision pierced the knee cap of the boy and he tumbled to the ground screeching.

Simon walked up to where Arnold lay. "You should have listened. We don't take the injured, they slow us down."

A deathly scream carried on the branches of the trees which made Willow shiver. She didn't have time to think about who it was. She had just found Diana, Faramund, Iskander and Zsiga. "Quickly this way," she said as they raced for the white stone building.

"Prince Simon over there," a man called out.

An arrow whizzed by her head just missing. Another hit a branch which moved to protect her. *'Almost there,'* she thought as an arrow hit Faramund in the shoulder. He stumbled and barely caught his footing, Willow grabbed his arm, pulled him along. She motioned behind them, sending tree branches flying at any enemies that followed. New trees began growing to block the path they were following. Her heart raced, she could feel the pounding in her throat. Her mouth was dry. At last she saw it. As they set foot in the clearing she knew they were safe for the moment. She flopped on the ground, breathing heavily.

"Gran!" Nathan exclaimed with joy as he ran into her arms.

Willow motioned to Jessie who came to help Faramund with his injury. He looked at her, his eyes longing to hear if she had found Victoria yet. She shook her head and headed back out to see if she could find his sister.

It wasn't long before she heard another scream. Willow rushed in the direction it came from and arrived in time to see a man firmly holding on Victoria's arm.

"I don't want to hurt you girl just come along quietly," he said.

A branch from the tree behind him swung straight at his legs. The man tumbled to the ground releasing the girl. Willow lunged forward and picked her up. Looking down at the man on the ground she was stunned for just a moment. She felt something move in her stomach and a lump form in her throat. His two bright blue eyes locked on hers. His jet black hair with blue highlights blew in the wind majestically. Willow had never seen a boy as beautiful as he was in that moment.

'Now?' Kiera's voice sounded knowing what Willow was feeling. *'Now you decide to get interested in boys and did it have to be the enemy? Really?'*

"Lance," a voice yelled out too close for comfort. That was enough day dreaming. She was gone in a flash. Behind her she heard, "What happened to you?" and a reply, "I didn't see a branch," before the voices faded out of her hearing range.

Up ahead she saw two figures standing over someone on the ground. She approached with caution but saw it was Malarchy and Jade. The boy on the ground was Arnold. There was nothing they could do for him. It was already too late.

'Could this day get any worse?' she thought to herself.

Shielding Victoria's face from the body on the ground, she passed by the two, paused for a moment before motioning to them to follow. They were only steps away from the building.

Victoria ran straight to her brothers and hugged them. When she had smothered all three thoroughly, she greeted the others, using her talents to heal anyone who had been hurt, as best she could. The rest of the group stood and stared in disbelief at the sight of Jade and her father. An awkward situation to say the least. The two had been at the very heart of the reason everyone was standing there right now.

"We can't leave them out there," Willow said knowing what everyone was thinking. Seeing the others weren't in agreement with her, she added, "They made wrong choices, I agree, but like any of us they can learn and change and they will have to carry the burden of what they have done with them for the rest of their lives. If we leave them out there, we will be making a wrong choice too, that we would have to live with."

"She is traumatized," Malarchy blurted out referring to his daughter. "She watched them kill her mother and take away her brother."

"A lot of people are dead or taken," Neil shouted back. It was the first time he had spoken since the invasion had begun.

"We have to do something to stop them," Malarchy pleaded.

It was Willow who responded with a touch of anger in her voice. "Look at us. We are all that are left. What do you suggest we do. They would wipe us out in a second. No, we are waiting until they go and then we can regroup and decide what can be done."

"I don't think that is an option," Malarchy said looking at the ground.

"What do you mean?"

He took in a large breath of air. "Joseph, one of the leaders, he told us he was leaving us behind to burn in some kind of fire...necrid flames is what he called it."

"Necrid flames are bad." Nathan stepped forward away from his Grandmother. "It's a blue flame that burns anything living. It makes ghost worlds. The direct opposite of terra forming. The flames keep burning until there is no more life...nothing else can extinguish it."

"We don't have much time left if they are heading back!" Malarchy exclaimed. "When they leave they will set the flames."

Clairity almost fell to her knees, "Ashlyn, she is hurt on the hill. She needs help."

"I will go," Willow started, turning her attention to her friend.

"No, I will. I have increased speed. I can make it faster. Just lead us back here once we get to the treeline," Jessie said.

"The trees will show you a path, I will meet you for the last part," Willow said. "Thank you."

Jessie ran to the hill racing against time.

"We need to find someway." Willow's thoughts exploded through all of the information that had bombarded her mind. *'Portals,'* she thought. *'All known portals closed...known portals...there must be a hidden portal...but how do we find it? Prophecies, there are prophecies about...'* "Diana would there be a book containing prophecies? I know some were only heard by the council, but other ones the keepers would have kept?"

"Yes, *'The Portal Prophecies'*. It's quite large," The historian replied.

"Nathan, have you seen it?" Willow said hoping the boy had read it already.

"No, I haven't," he replied.

"Where haven't you read books yet?" Willow asked.

He pointed to a section on the opposite semi circle to where he was standing.

"Quickly, I need to find this book. Only look for the very largest books."

Clairity had found it before she had even finished speaking. "I had a feeling," she said.

Placing it on the stone table Willow turned to Diana again, "This is your writing. You recorded all of these as historian. Is there somewhere, a prophecy about the blue flame?"

Mrs. Waddington looked as if a light had gone off inside her head. "Yes, yes there is!" She turned the pages of the book, when she stopped she read out loud...

"When the blue flames engulf the land, only one whose will is steadied, by that discovered can break that which is set in stone to escape."

She heard Jessie call and ran out to meet him. He was carrying Ashlyn. They joined the others and watched as Willow paced back and forth repeating the prophecy.

What did it mean, her mind raced, "Somethings only you can discover...an ability it has to be...break that which is set in stone...in stone." She looked at the book on the table. She moved the book and handed it to Clairity to hold, then ran her fingers over the four corners of the table.

"Shouldn't we try to do something?" Malarchy yelled. "We are out of time."

"She is trying to do something," Clairity replied. "Let her concentrate."

Willow looked up and for the first time and noticed above the stone table there was an opening. A small square that let the light shine down on the table.

She turned to Ashlyn. "The dreams...in our dreams, there was a giant storm, it was in the other prophecy as well about today. Everything else has happened, but the great storm...the thunder and..." her words cut off. She understood.

"Stand back everyone inside one of the two side rooms against the walls. Don't lose that book Clairity." Willow yelled.

Raising her hands to the sky and looking upward a gold dust appeared flowing from her hands. The clouds swirled above, rain fell heavier than they had seen it before. The winds howled and within seconds thunder boomed through the air. A single bolt of lightening struck the table, breaking it into pieces and the four corner stones broke loose flying into position as if drawn by a magnet. A portal opened before them with a rainbow of lights in the middle.

"Go," Willow screamed. The necrid flames were almost upon them. She watched as each of the survivors ran through, then jumped through herself with only seconds to spare, not knowing where they would end up on the other side.

King Cornelius

The three princes returned to their homeland. Here, whether day or night, the skies were orange with red highlights and purple clouds. Red sands covered much the world, bordering on seas of black liquid where some of the most vicious sea creatures ever to live called home. Towns scattered along the shore lines of the seas, housing the population not enlisted in aiding the war efforts. Fishermen would risk their lives to capture any one of the deadly water creatures, which when cooked properly, were considered a delicacy by the King, and worth more riches than could be earned in any other trade.

In the centre of the land was a great mountain of black rock. A Castle was carved into the rock itself. One lone path rounded up the sides, with several large platforms of flat sheet rock along the way, leading to a gate at the top which allowed entrance. This area was the living quarters and King's Court. Under the main levels, buried deep in the mountain were the servants' quarters, below that the dungeons, filled with all sorts of beings, captured from different worlds. Some would be made to join the army, others were to be studied, exploited for whatever was to the use or need of the King or his children.

The black forest bordered the foot of the mountain, filled with large dark trees, which in any other world may appear as dead or dying. They had no leaves, and stood silent. Several large branches exploded from the top and grew downwards, each dividing into five separate vine like branches, resembling large hands with long fingers. The finger like vines could sense movement and wrap around any living thing, pulling the poor creature to its base where the bark of the tree would open and surround its prey, absorbing the very essence of its life.

There was one road through the forest which was used by tradesmen, hunters and fisherman, at their own risk, to bring their items to a market place located on the first stone platform heading up the mountain. The other platforms all contained vast amounts of housing for the King's armies.

Today the halls of the castle echoed with laughter and celebration for the victories the Princes and Princesses were to bestowed upon their father.

"A toast to Prince Joseph, Prince Simon and Prince Lance, for the conquest of yet another world. Come my sons. Tell me tales of today's adventures," the King's voice trumpeted as he raised a glass of wine in the air, its precious liquid overflowing in every direction he turned.

"A perfectly flawless attack, no injuries except for Lance, he picked a fight with a tree and lost ending on his backside," Joseph answered laughing.

"To be fair the tree was twice my size," Lance answered with a smile. "And nothing was hurt but my pride."

"Do we know the name of the world you so boldly conquered?" Cornelius asked.

"No father, but one of our new guests will be willing to share I am sure." Joseph was the most ruthless of the three princes. He executed his father's requests without question and was quick to claim the glory as well.

"Casualties?" One of the King's royal eyebrows raised a the query.

"Limited, a few struggled and were executed or left behind," Joseph answered.

"Without knowing what world this is? I explicitly instructed you that I am looking for someone. How do you know she wasn't one of your casualties?" the King yelled, a blush red colour creeping up his cheeks.

"I highly doubt this was that world father. There was nothing but a small town of wooden huts and one castle. Even the prisoner count is minimal."

"Find out quickly about this world. Ask the captives the names of who is missing so I can be sure." Cornelius turned to Lance. "The necrid flames? They have been lit?"

"Yes, the world should be consumed by now and barren of all life, useless to anyone ever again," Lance replied.

"Your gift is a blessing my son. Soon we shall have destroyed all of those who imprisoned us and the walls they built, not just around us but around thousands of worlds. They imposed their will on us unjustly, took our friends and relatives, turned them against us and had them betray us. They told us we were not good enough for their utopia and denied us the right to make our own."

"Have my sisters returned?" Prince Joseph asked.

"Not yet," the King answered. "When they do we shall celebrate till the morning. Till then perhaps you can work on a few of our new guests, find some information."

"As you wish, my King," Joseph answered and turned to the staircase leading down to the dungeons.

The stone staircase was dark and cold. The three princes headed down past the servants' quarters, past the next two levels which housed beings who were being reformed or chose to join the King's army and were in training, to the very lower level dungeons. Here there were several different rooms which spread across a few levels, including interrogation rooms and holding cells all carved from rock and virtually escape free.

"Bets? I think I can crack one first," Simon said with a smile.

Joseph smiled. "Brotherly competition, my favourite."

"I will sit this one out, you two enjoy," Lance replied. "I may visit some old...friends." The prince disappeared into the deepest darkest part of the castle's lower levels.

The first two holding cells were full of the new guests to the castle. Simon chose a young girl to interrogate, motioning a guard to have her brought to a private room.

"Hello," Simon said smiling. He was able to turn on the charm when he wanted to on the same level as Joseph. In fact women found all three of the princes to be irresistible. They were all handsome, tall, well built, and eloquent speakers. "I am Prince Simon and you are?"

"Sabrina," the girl answered in a shaky voice.

"Sabrina, very nice to meet your acquaintance. I believe there has been a misunderstanding, I want to fix things, but to do so, I need your help. The sooner I sort through the answers, the sooner we can improve your situation here. Okay?"

"I am not sure what help I can be. I don't know anything," she answered.

Simon laughed. "I haven't asked anything yet so how could you know whether or not you know? These questions aren't difficult. They are about your home. For instance what was the name of your town and world?"

"Name? It didn't have a name, at least not one I have ever heard. It was just our home. We didn't speak of other places." Her voice shook in fear that her answer might anger the man before her.

"No name at all? There was only the one town and it had no name either?" Simon asked.

"Just the one town. I don't think we ever needed it to have a name, or maybe '*the town*' was its name," she answered.

"Okay," he said smiling. "It makes sense, there was no need...there are some people missing correct? Do you think you could name them?"

"Yes there are some. Why do you want to know who they are?"

"Like I said, this is I believe a terrible mistake, I just need to rule out the person we are looking for wasn't hiding in your town," he answered convincingly.

"Hiding? Like a criminal? Odd things were happening lately. Do you think that is why? This person was scared you were coming for them?"

"Yes...yes, it most likely is. Why don't you tell me the names so we can try to bring this evil person to justice?" Simon listened and wrote down all the names. "That's all, you are sure?"

"Yes...wait I almost forgot. Diana and thinking back, she had been taken away bound with ropes by the castle guards for something she had done."

The young prince's face went white. "What did she look like?"

"Tall, thin, very pristine, hair always very neat, tied back in a bun, clothes always clean and proper. Nice features, some of the girls wished they had her cheek bones. She was pleasant to look at and well spoken. Is it her?" Sabrina asked, without hesitation.

"I don't know," he answered leaving the room to find his brother.

Joseph had chosen a woman from the town named Martha, but hadn't gotten very far. He was about to slap the woman for the fourth time for not answering his questions, when Simon flung open the door asking to speak to him. After leaving the room, he listened to the story and read the names on the list, which was a little more extensive than he had expected.

"There are many worlds brother. I am sure there are many women by the same name as our long lost Aunt. The whole thing seems unlikely, don't you think?" Joseph asked.

"How so?" Simon asked.

"Guardians were creatures of great power. When they separated the worlds to their own taste and created their utopia, do you think they would have designed beaten up old wooden shacks for their keepers to live in? Our dungeons have better accommodations. Also, wouldn't there have been a guardian or two left to protect their homeland? No, I think this was a trial colony of some sort, an experiment. The size of the world itself was so small, one town, no bodies of water. Surely a powerful ancient race would have made a better home for itself." Joseph motioned to one of his men to return the captives to the holding cells with the others.

"Wait!" Simon smiled. "The girl in the other room, have the maids bathe her and find her something...appealing to wear, then bring her to my room to wait for me. I do enjoy celebrations."

Joseph laughed. "Let's find Lance."

Lance was on the very lowest level of the dungeon when his two brothers found him. He had been standing in front of a special rock enclosure which was clear to see through and naturally blocked many special abilities. Inside was a woman with light strawberry coloured curly hair, shades paler than the girl he had seen in the forest earlier. They had similar facial features, perhaps related he thought. He hadn't been able to get the vision of the girl out of his mind. She was different some how, something about her intrigued him like no other girl had before. His thoughts were interrupted.

"Something wrong?" Joseph asked handing him the list of names that had been collected.

"No, just wondering how to get her to give up the other creature," Lance lied while looking over the list.

"Why? The other one is immortal. We have eternity to torture it for its crimes," Simon offered.

"It no longer responds. Look for yourself. I think it is broken beyond repair, as good as dead but trapped in life. It has given up and is useless to you now," Lance responded.

Joseph entered the cell beside the woman his brother was watching and returned with a body of a black bird, motionless. One wing had been removed, all of its bones had been repeatedly broken. It had endured the worst forms of torture until it could endure no more.

"Immortal isn't always a blessing," Joseph mused.

A loud noise came from down the hallway. Three girls, all dressed in black, their skin a pale olive green were heading their way.

"Do we have victory sisters?" Joseph asked.

"Victory...there was nothing to be victorious over. This was the first world we have seen with no intelligent life forms. At first we thought there were some humanoids but it ended up being just bunch of beasts, sharp teeth and claws...vicious yes...but usable, no. The land however, was perfect to assimilate into the new world once the barriers between space come down. We made sure any plant life would die off quickly and water sources would dry up fast. It won't be long before it is barren land that we can later transform into whatever we want," Zoe responded. She was the impulsive one of the three princesses, quick to make decisions. "I thought those things couldn't die," she added referring to the bird her brother was holding.

"They can't but it is broken, beyond help now. I just don't know what to do with it. Seems such a waste to use valuable space on it now," Joseph answered.

Without a word Zoe grabbed the bird and rushed back up the staircase. Several minutes later she returned smiling.

"What did you do?" Lance asked.

"The doorway was still open to the world we were just in. I threw it in. Let the beasts play with it some before they expire and it's out of our hair. We can use that room for other things now," she answered.

"I may be starting to understand why you are father's favourite Zoe," Joseph said.

"Why don't you share the good news with the lady, Lance. I am sure it will jolt her some, maybe even anger her enough to let the other one out to play," Simon said.

"Actually, I think I will have a chat with her and catch up to you later at the celebration." Lance entered the stone room and closed the door behind him.

"Hello," Lance said. He had never actually paid any attention to the women before. "Raven, isn't it?"

"I have no inclination to speak with you," she snapped.

"I have information for you, about your friend and...daughter," Lance said.

Raven's eyes widened, "What has happened to the guardian? Return her to me and we can speak."

"I am afraid I can't. The guardian gave up hope. The torture you let it endure on your behalf was too much for it to bare. The broken body was discarded moments ago."

"You are a vile race, without any signs of morals or decency," she yelled, spitting in the prince's face.

Lance took a cloth from his pocket and wiped his face. "It was your precious guardians who imposed their will on us. They took our lands, our property, our family and our right to grow away from us. They imprisoned us with walls created between worlds, designed to hold us back from our true potential. We are not the villains here we are the victims. If you are as civilized as you pretend then why weren't we consulted as to our future?"

"Your father was angry, furious, his sister was chosen by guardians to help in the restructuring and he was not. That is what you fight for, a man's jealousy," she cried turning away.

"And you? What do you fight for? Your daughter? No, you left her...didn't you?" Lance was fishing for information, anything he could find out about the girl from the forest. Could she have escaped? Would he meet her again? His blood rushed through his body at the thought, blue flames blazing in his eyes.

"What are you looking for prince?" Raven asked as if reading his thoughts. Perhaps the clear rock wasn't as good an ability blocker as had been thought.

"Her name," he answered honestly.

"I must disappoint you then. I have no daughter...If I did, her name would never cross your lips, that I would make sure," Raven said.

"Your world was destroyed by necrid flames a few hours ago. Tell me did she have the talent to escape?"

"Nothing can escape necrid flames. Is that not true?"

Lance smiled, she had given him all the information he wanted. The look in her eyes told him the girl was her daughter, and her lack of concern meant she was alive somewhere. Their paths would cross again one day, and he looked forward to the confrontation it would bring.

Chapter Sixteen

Willow landed with a thud, banging her head on something on the ground. Years of being joined with several Leanders, the cat like race of ancient beings, meant she had picked up a few of their traits including night vision, stealth, agility and she had always landed on her feet, at least before now. There had been no choice but to leap head first through the portal as the necrid flames engulfed the forest around them and even less time to worry about how she would land on the other side or what she would find. Rubbing her head she realized she had hit it on the book she had asked Clairity not to lose, *'The Portal Prophecies.'* Without that book she never would have figured out how to escape in the first place. She looked up to see if the others were okay, but it wasn't a friend that greeted her.

A weapon, some form of a gun that she and Nathan had read about in one of the weapons encyclopedias they had found, was pointed in her face. This day just wasn't going to end she thought to herself.

"Get up," a male voice said.

Willow got to her feet. She staggered a bit, the bump on her head had made her dizzy. Looking at her captor she couldn't tell much other than he was a tall man. He wore a baseball cap that hid the features of his face from her.

"Turn around," the man ordered.

Willow faced her back to the stranger, trying to search for signs of her friends who had come through the portal before her.

"Hi, I'm..."

The stranger cut her off, "Don't speak, we know about your kind and what you are looking for."

"My kind? What kind?" she said.

"I said no speaking," he repeated. "Now just walk over there and join the others you came with till we can figure out what you are doing here."

"Might be easier to figure that out if I could talk." she said under her breath, but loud enough that her captor could hear.

"Just shut up, okay? Don't get me mad," he barked back.

"Okay, okay. Just saying, you can't know what we are doing here, if we are the only ones who know and you won't let us tell you."

"Enough, I am not listening to your tricks," he yelled.

'Real winner this one is,' Kiera said telepathically.

'Can you see him, what he looks like?' Willow asked in her mind.

'No, we can do a lot of things but seeing through a jacket isn't one of them,' Aslo answered.

'Right, forgot I was still wearing it,' she answered silently.

Ahead of her she could see the others now. They all seemed fine, at least for the moment. There were several men with guns keeping them in a line. She took the place beside her best friend, Clairity.

"Well this is much better," Malarchy whispered.

"You could have stayed and fried in the flames, pretty sure I didn't twist your arm," Willow whispered back. Malarchy and his daughter had little right to complain. They were right at the heart of the actions that led up to what had happened.

"Can you ever be quiet?" the stranger's voice asked.

A few of her friends in the group let out a little giggle forcing Willow to peak her head down the line and ask, "Really?"

"Hello, man with a gun here. Just shut up," the stranger said, a strong sense of authority resonated in his voice.

"Yes, yes, scarey man with weapon. I am just a little confused. You...want us to stand here until what? You magically figure out how and why we are here?" Willow asked.

"You left out without speaking." He added, "It's been a bad day, don't test me."

Willow chuckled. "Wanna compare notes?"

"Someone get some duct tape for her mouth please," the stranger yelled to the other men.

One of the men ran to a truck. She recognized it from the pictures drawn in one of the books Nathan had shared with her. This world used them for transportation. She found the idea fascinating, to have so much space that they needed to use something to move them from one spot to another. It had to be huge or people would just walk. When the man returned, he was carrying something round and silver. He pulled part of it and it seemed to stretch, then rip. He placed it over her mouth. It stuck. Her mouth was stuck shut. She tried to move her lips but nothing '*mmmmmmmummm*' was the type of noise she could make. '*How rude,*' she thought.

Time seemed to go by slowly. Willow tried to complain a few times but her muffled sounds just made the stranger laugh. When she looked at the others to say something she ended up just sighing. It was clear none of them wanted to have the stuff put over their mouths. Of course she couldn't blame them for that. It was uncomfortable and irritating. She wasn't sure how long she had been standing there before another truck pulled up and a man stepped out. Her captors seemed to have their own little meeting. Then the new man moved in front of her group.

"Who is in charge?" he asked.

No one moved or talked. The stranger moved to Willow's side, pushed her away from the others, then pulled the sticky stuff off her face in one swift motion.

"Owe!" Willow screamed. "That hurt, You really have some nerve. You can't just go around gluing people's mouths shut like that!"

"This one should have no problem answering questions," he said. "We should talk here where the others can't hear."

"Perhaps I don't want to answer your questions now!" Willow said crossing her arms across her chest.

"Oh, I think your need to speak will take over without problem," he said with a chuckle.

"Enough!" The man who had just arrived raised his hand in a stop motion. On his arm he had a picture Willow had seen before.

"You are a portal guard?" she asked.

"My name is William and I am the one asking questions. Who might you be?"

"Willow," she answered. "Are you all portal guards?"

"No, and I am asking questions, remember?" he said.

"Yes but seems strange if you are a portal guard and they aren't, why were they at the portal and you weren't?" she asked.

"It's a long story, but I need to know who you are and why you are here," he said.

"Why should we trust you?" she answered. "You capture us, point weapons at us, refuse to listen to our story, put stuff over my mouth, then want to know everything."

William was starting to get frustrated. "You recognized the symbol on my arm, and you seem to know what it means, that tells you what I am..."

She cut off his words. "And three of us have that same mark. Did anyone trust them? Or extend hospitality? I can answer that...No."

William looked at the stranger, "Is that true Mike?"

"I didn't look," he said. "They were all just sneaking around, so we rounded them up and waited for you."

"The book might have been a give away." She held up the large book she was still carrying titled '*The Portal Prophecies*'.

Mike shrugged. "I thought it was one of those conspiracy books that keep popping up. This group looks like a bunch of groupie wannabes looking for a supernatural thrill."

William walked over to the others and asked to see a portal guard symbol on any of their arms. The three guards stepped forward and put their arms together so all the pictures were beside each other matching perfectly. William dismissed his other men and led the group to a house, about a five minute walk away.

Outside the cabin type building, more men and women were stationed each carrying weapons similar to the ones the men in the forest had and positioned at fairly even intervals from one another.

Inside, the main room had a couch, some chairs and floor pillows all situated around a fireplace, which was lit and heated the room to a balmy temperature. To the back was a separate space just enough room for a wooden table and chairs.

William and Mike motioned to most of the group to sit down in front of the fireplace and had the guards follow them to the table. Willow took it upon herself to join them.

"Why don't you sit with the others?" Mike motioned to Willow.

She looked at him, then William, then the guards. Faramund had a smile on his face and was trying not to laugh. She turned around and faced Mike. "I think I am more qualified to be at this table than you are."

William laughed. "There will be time for argument, but for now if we could sit down maybe we could find out what is going on."

"I only know parts of the back story about the ongoing war with the Serpent Ancients, the Xiuhcoatle and the prophecies." Willow paused.

"What happened tonight? What brought you here is what we are most curious about," William said still smiling.

Zsiga responded. "Our world was invaded and destroyed. We are all that escaped death or capture. We are the last of our kind."

"Forgive me if I don't look surprised, but we had written off our home world long ago when no further reinforcements were sent." William's facial expression embodied all the qualities of a boy who had just lost his best friend.

"Communication was lost and the council feared the worst," the head guard responded.

"That we can explain, the serpents and their allies found a way to weaken the space between the worlds, in short punching holes in them," William said leaning back in his chair so that the two front legs lifted off the ground.

Mike picked up the story. "Some of your portals when active created a strain on the weakened space, so the forces you had left here at the time, disabled them and hid the stones needed to activate them again. That way no further damage could be done."

"So, we lost contact because you disabled some of the portals disrupting the telepathic connection?" Willow asked.

"You catch on fast. A guardian could still open a portal from the other side to move through, but they closed after use. No one did," Mike replied.

"They separated our forces. I am the last guard left in the this world. These men and women, working with me, are individuals whose lives were touched by the war, they have lost family and friends and joined the cause to help protect this world. They are good people but we are losing the battle. Perhaps with your help we can hold on a bit longer," William said.

"With the portals closed, what are you fighting?" Willow asked.

"Not all the portals are inactive. There are a few we monitor. There are also a few rogue holes in space that have been created, that we don't know how to repair. All manor of beings have come through. From what we know they open and close on their own and only for a certain amount of time."

"We are lucky this world has an imagination and loves conspiracy theories. They make their own stories up about everything that happens. A few rumours in the right ear and they cover it up for us. That's what we thought your group was, thrill seekers looking for proof of something or anything." Mike added, "Sorry about that."

Willow didn't believe at all he was sorry. There was something about his sheepish grin that said he had enjoyed annoying her.

"It's late and most of us have had too much excitement for today. Would you mind if we slept here?" she asked.

"Of course, we have extra buildings with beds that are all empty at the moment. Mike can get you all settled and tomorrow we will show you around," William answered. "Tomorrow perhaps you can explain how you opened a sealed portal."

"Easy," Willow said. "I read the book." She pushed the prophecies book across the table.

Mike showed them round back of the house where there were a series of additional buildings. They were directed to the third building. Inside were beds with full body cushions, evenly spaced throughout the main room. Each bed had a storage chest and a small closet for personal items. Mike informed them this was their own place since no one else was staying there and showed them the bathrooms and showers.

"Someone will be by in the morning to show you the rest of the facility," Mike said. "You should be safe here. The patrols are out."

Before Willow and the others could thank him, a gun shot sounded in the distance, followed by some shouting.

"Stay here and lock the door. Don't open it for anyone," Mike yelled as he ran out towards the sound of another gun firing.

Malarchy bolted forward and locked the door, then moved away from it and began checking the windows to make sure they were all also locked.

"What are you doing? We should try to help." Willow wasn't sure what the noises outside were about but she was certain someone could be hurt and need their help.

"We don't even know what we would be up against and we don't know anything about this world. We need to wait till morning," he replied sternly.

"As much as I hate to say it Malarchy is right. We can take shifts sleeping until day light and hopefully someone sends for us." Zsiga was already setting up with the other two guards to have at least one of them awake at all times till morning.

Willow sat down on a bed and Clairity joined her. "They are right you know, we will be more help in the morning. I have that feeling."

"Thanks." Willow smiled at her friend's words. Clairity's intuition had been bang on these past few days.

"One thing I wanted to ask you, back at the stone table, why didn't Kiera and Aslo just tell you how to escape? We almost died."

Willow took a big breath and let it out while trying to find the words to explain. "Because...there are some things I needed to find out for myself...When I read the prophecy, I knew I could do it. I had never used anywhere near that amount of power before...but I knew I could. If someone had of just told me I could, there would have been doubt. I wouldn't have believed in myself enough to create the force that was needed."

"I get it." Her friend smiled. "Best we get some sleep, tomorrow I think may be a full day."

Willow laid down. Sleep wasn't going to be easy. What was out there? Would there be anyone left to come for them in the morning?

Chapter Seventeen

A loud knock on the door jolted Willow awake. She wasn't sure how long she had been asleep, but it wasn't long, the yelling outside had continued through the night. Iskander opened the door, letting Mike in. With daylight shining in the windows, she was able to see more of his features. His hair was cut very short and if it were longer she imagined it would be a similar colour to her own. His eyes were a dull green which matched the clothes he was wearing. From the dark circles around his eyes, she could tell he had had little sleep last night as well.

"We have arranged an escort for you back to the main building. Bring anything you need. You won't be back here again till later tonight," Mike said to the guard, his voice loud enough for everyone to hear.

There wasn't anytime to think. The escort was waiting and they were on their way within minutes to hopefully some answers about last night.

When they arrived at the room they had been in the previous night, it looked completely different. It had been transformed into a command centre. There were large boards with maps and coloured flags inserted at different points. Men and women were buzzing around with hand held devices they were talking through. One woman with her hair tied back in a neat bun wearing all green the same colour as Mike's shirt, was pinning more flags in several of the maps. William was going over more maps at the table. He looked up and brushed the hair from his eyes, with a smile he extended an invitation to join him at the table.

"Sorry things are a bit crazy round here today. We had a...well problem arise last night."

"What happened?" Willow asked. "Maybe we could help. It doesn't look like you have solved the problem yet."

"Best you stay here where you won't get hurt and let the experts handle this," Mike answered.

William shook his head still smiling. "The opening of the portal you came through created one of those holes we told you about and a dozen or so creatures managed to come through, maybe more. We haven't seen anything like them before. We don't even know what world they came from."

"What did they look like?" she asked.

"Humanoid, pale greyish skin, razor sharp teeth, hands and feet looked more paw-like than human and the females appeared to have wings of some sort. Rather ugly really, but super fast and deadly," Mike answered.

"Hannulate!" Nathan said.

"Sounds like it," Willow agreed. "They were once one of the most beautiful races to exist. They were peaceful and fun loving creatures who lived in magical realms. A direct cousin to faeries and pixies."

"That doesn't sound much like the creatures I described," Mike snorted.

"Because they changed. During the blood wars an evil king captured them, all of them, the entire race. Kept in chains in a dismal dungeon, they were tortured but kept alive to harvest their blood to fuel the kingdom's war. Their species has a unique ability to adapt, and they did just that, developing sharp teeth and razor claws that could extend at will and strong enough to cut the chains that bound them. Then one night, while the armies were away waging war to acquire more possessions, they escaped and murdered any person they met.

They considered all humans a threat, and probably still do. It took less than an hour for them to wipe out the entire kingdom."

"Great...any good news?" William asked.

"Yes, and no. They are at the moment nocturnal and during the day they will want to hide and rest. You have a window of opportunity to find them in day light."

"And the bad news?"

"I told you they adapt, it won't be long before the day light won't bother them anymore. Then they will be harder to track," she answered.

"Except by following the body count," Mike added. "We need to double up the search now, call everyone back, double shifts till dusk. Let's destroy them before nightfall," Mike said speaking to the men and women waiting for instructions around them.

"Destroy them?" Willow shrieked. "No, you can't! It isn't their fault."

"They are killing people. We should just let them?" Mike argued.

"Did anyone try talking to them? Did you even listen to what they have been through? People made them this way. They adapted to being abused, in order to survive. With a little compassion they could change back into the beautiful creatures they were meant to be." Willow was now directly facing Mike and the two were standing only inches apart from each other as if having their own argument and no one else existed.

William cut in, "This isn't a capture operation Willow. Even if we could, what would we do with them? They pose a threat to everyone around. We aren't going to take that chance. They will be destroyed and people of this world will be safe."

Willow heard a gasp from Kiera. She didn't even have to think what it meant, she knew. "When did you change our purpose?" Willow asked with tears swelling in her eyes.

"Hope this place is rain proof," Malarchy said to Diana. Willow hadn't noticed the comment she was too involved in what was happening. Malarchy was right of course, the clouds were forming outside, rain was ready to pour down on them.

"What do you mean?" William asked moving closer to her, looking as if he was angry at being accused of something. Faramund moved to Willow's side, poised to protect her at all costs.

"I mean the guardians meant to protect all worlds and all creatures, not just this one and these people. As portal guards you defend against threats yes, but these beings didn't choose to come here. They didn't come through the portal to attack. They are victims. Yet you feel you have the right to condemn them, judge them and sentence them. That isn't and never was our birth right and purpose," Willow said not backing down.

"Look around little girl, this isn't a game. I am all that is left. These people are here helping me hold on, to protect this world. They didn't sign up for guardian philosophy 101. Without them I would be gone by now and then there wouldn't have been any of us left in this world." William anger raged, blood rushing to his face turning it bright red.

"You aren't one of us," Willow said wishing she hadn't. But she was right, he had forsaken the duty he was bound to for the well being of one world and had been doing so for sometime.

"What do you know about it? What makes you the expert on what the guardians would approve of?" he snapped.

"I know the mark on your arm is fading as we speak. I know you could be removed of your duty if you do this," Willow said echoing Aslo's words in her mind.

William looked at his arm. What had once been a dark blue had faded to a light baby blue. He looked perplexed. "I have had this policy for sometime now. Why all of a sudden?" His words faded off.

"I guess you didn't notice until now. It was probably a subtle change taking place over time." Willow heard Aslo's voice again and relayed his message. "I believe you will find it will darken again should you chose the path you were meant to follow."

William looked hurt. He moved to the table and sat down. "We have done our best here. It hasn't been easy."

"I am sure it hasn't, but our best isn't always what is right. These creatures deserve a chance and I plan to try." She turned her attention to the others. "Nathan can you take a yellow flag and mark on the map where the portal to their homeland is please." Turning back to William she asked, "Is the portal at that location active?"

Mike looked at the placement of the flag pin on the map. "Yes the pink flags are known closed portals. That one, if it is there hasn't been discovered yet."

"Okay, so all we need to do is round them up and send them home," she said.

"You forget they are savage," Mike said.

"You forget they are beings who have great intelligence. They learnt to be savage from men in order to survive. Part of them can still be reasoned with," Willow said. "We can divide into three teams, two search parties and one to remain here. Nathan and Diana, can you two complete that map with each of the portals that are missing?"

Nathan and Diana agreed. Willow was about to split up the teams, when Mike interrupted, "I do hate to butt in and all...actually no I don't. You arrive here after how many thousands of years, waltz in, insult the man who has dedicated his life to protecting a portal and preserving life here and try to take over? This man watched everyone he knows disappear or die. This isn't your show, so back off!"

Silence over came the room as everyone stopped what they were doing and were staring, waiting for new instructions from, someone. Willow looked at William sitting at the table alone with his hands on his face, elbows on the table. As much as she hated to admit it Mike was right. This was William's place, his army, his supplies, it was his show. They needed to agree. She asked everyone to clear the room for a few minutes so she could talk to the guard alone. William looked up and nodded to his people to step outside.

"I am sorry. I was wrong to take over like that. I will prepare to leave immediately. Most of my people will join me, however a few may prefer to remain in your hospitality. They won't interfere with your operations."

"How do you know all this? That what I am doing isn't what I was meant to do? That the mark will reappear?" William asked his head hung low facing the table.

"I..." Willow felt a tug in her left shoulder. Seconds later a black cat jumped on the table and sat looking at the guard.

"I am Aslo, Leander and guardian, I spoke the words to the girl. She is my keeper. She only repeated what I asked her to."

Both William and Willow gasped out loud as if they were seeing a ghost. Silence followed for several minutes before Aslo spoke again.

"We don't have time for this, daylight hours are passing and there is work to be done. You are a good guard William, but your path has been lost over the years. Not just one world has the right to survive, they all do. We do not have the right to judge how they live. Our job is simply to ensure they have the right to live as they choose."

"It isn't always that simple," William said without emotion. "To protect one means to destroy another in some cases."

"Yes, there is no exact science, but we must try rather than just condemn. There are cases where the innocent must be defended and others destroyed, but in this case both parties are innocent. They both are fighting to exist and neither one has more right than the other to survive."

"I understand and will step aside."

"No!" Willow exclaimed. "These people look to you for direction. You need to lead them. We will do as you request. Ask us to leave or stay and help. I must follow the way of the guardians, but I will respect your choice."

"What do I...we do? How do we save both?"

"We try," Willow answered. "First of course we have to find them."

William gave a half smile. "Yeah, that should be easy enough."

"We do have some skill sets that may help a little," Willow said sensing the sarcasm in his voice.

"I forgot completely about that. I have a unique radar to locate portal stones within walking distance of me. I expect you each have something different."

"You could say that, but for the moment we are out of time. We need to find the missing Hannulate and get them home before more damage is done," Aslo said as he jumped to Willow's shoulder and disappeared onto the surface of her skin again.

Chapter Eighteen

William got up from the table and summoned the others back into the room, giving a short speech that all had been worked out and a common goal had been found. The details of which would be made known later after the urgency of the day had been settled.

Tactical teams were formed. William headed the first, picking several of his own men as well as Iskander, Jessie, Dezi and Pete to cover ground to the north. Willow was to lead the second group to the south, consisting of Mike, Faramund, Zsiga, and Neil.

The remainder of the people were to remain at the base of operations, some to protect, and some in the command centre.

Nathan, Diana, Ashlyn and Clairity were assigned to helping the young girl who maintained the maps, Sarah. Over the course of the morning they heard her story about how she had lost her parents and younger siblings to the vamprite, a race she knew as vampires. Back in the time of the blood wars when humanoids were looking to drink the blood of the magic folk, a young prince, Drake, decided turn about was fair play. He captured young women and drank their blood. It was soon learnt that drinking human blood could keep his race of shape shifters young, strong, and beautiful. Given the chance the vamprite would gladly invade and live in this world. They had once before found a foothold here. It was believed a few hundred had come through one of the holes in space between realms and had taken up residence. It was easy to understand the folk lore people had built up about vampires and why cover-ups weren't a problem in this world. The people here made up stories to explain the unknown themselves.

Their job was to fill in information Nathan had read in books about portal locations and which worlds they connected to on the maps. Sarah was also marking whether individual portals had been disabled or not and any information about where portal stones were hidden that she knew.

The rest were given communication devices to stay in contact with the two groups. The guards themselves could stay updated since they could communicate telepathically.

Within moments the groups were prepped and on their way. The command centre was busy locating possibilities for dark places where the creatures could hide for the groups to search.

Willow's group took the truck south, agreeing the possibilities were best that the Hannulate would have travelled at least to dense forest land, as there weren't any mountains or caves in their direction, as there were to the north.

The trees were tall and reminded her a little of home, although packed much tighter together. Willow had the urge to take off her shoes and climb. Being able to communicate with trees meant she could run across the top of the forest, feeling the branches and leaves beneath her bare feet and never worry about falling or hurting herself. She put her hand on the trunk of the tree in front of her and felt the warm whisper of welcome vibrate through her body. A feeling of complete relaxation came over her body. She was safe, protected, loved. Taking a rhythmic breath in and letting it out, she closed her eyes and saw what the trees had seen, where the beings they were looking for had gone. She thanked them and turned to the others in her search party.

"They aren't far. There is a dark spot in the forest where they stopped for rest. We can be there in less than ten minutes," Willow said to her team.

"Great, lead the way," Mike answered.

"I don't have to, we just follow the path."

Mike's eyes widened with surprise as the trees appeared to part in front him creating a dirt trail through the dense forest. He looked at Willow as if he was going to speak, but ended up shaking his head as he stepped forward to take the lead.

The trail ended at the darkest part of the forest. Mike stopped and turned to Willow as if questioning where to go, but not wanting to speak out loud and disturb the creatures he was sure were resting near by.

Moving forward, Willow placed her hand on a tree. Within moments branches of all the surrounding trees swayed and parted, revealing camouflaged bodies scattered on the ground like fallen leaves. The creature closest to her opened an eye and seeing the strangers, titled its head upward with a growl, showing off its sharp teeth. Seconds later it was on two feet and threatening attack. The wild war noises spitting from its jaws quickly awoke the others from their slumber and Willow's team found them face to face with danger.

"We mean you no harm. We want to help you return to your world," Willow said showing both hands in front of her with palms forward.

"Why should we trust you? We have been tricked by the humans before," it hissed.

A black cat appeared by Willow's feet, rubbing against her legs. The creature turned its attention to the animal.

"So, there is hope left then. We understood you were all...disposed of," it said still with more of a hissing noise than normal speech.

Kiera looked up and jumped forward, transforming into the largest animal Willow had ever seen. She had just assumed the guardian's normal form was that of a cat. Now Kiera was standing before her, towering well over her height, with a face similar to a black panther but a larger body, more like a black lion, if a lion came in an extra extra large size.

Kiera spoke. "As you can see, we are not and our keeper isn't either. We will help you return to your home. The humans in this place are not the same ones who hurt you in the past. They are helping us return order. We ask your friendship and trust and offer ours in return."

"Where were all of you when we were being tortured for generations? We had no friends then!" it exclaimed angrily.

"We did not know what had happened to your people. But now we wish to make sure that no atrocities like that happen to other races. There are fewer of us now, but our duty remains to protect the innocent," Kiera answered calmly, flicking her long tail back and forth.

"Then you are late. Our world was invaded today, It has been left barren of all water and plant life. There is nothing for us there. You cannot help us."

"We can still help you, more than you know. There is a terra former in our company, who can rebuild what was destroyed, perhaps even better than before."

"That is an unusual ability, very powerful, it is. Show us if you wish us to believe." Another creature from the back had moved forward to join in the conversation. "Perhaps an apple tree? We have not had food for some time."

Willow stepped forward and looked at the ground space available. "We will need a clear area. There is no room here for a full grown tree."

"I can transport us to a location close to the portal if I am allowed," Faramund offered.

"The others of your kind, you will help us to convince them as well? They separated from you in the other direction."

"And you know where they are? We will permit you to transport us and show us the power, then we will talk about other details. If you lie we...take action," a third creature spoke.

Kiera nodded and Faramund asked everyone to gather together in a group before him. He raised his arms and a green fog released from his palms. The coloured gas swirled around them and created a wall, above, below, beside. They could see nothing but green. The guard said the approximate coordinates of the portal to the creatures' homeland and seconds later the gas was retreating, back into Faramund's hands and a new scenery unfolded before their eyes.

They were within walking distance to the portal now, about five minutes away and in an open area, with no signs of human life to the eye. Willow stepped forward away from the group and asked a apple tree to grow for her. A small green sprout appeared, slowly getting larger. The group watched as the seedling transformed into a fully grown apple tree, then with blossoms and finally with red apples, sparkling in the sunlight.

Sunlight, Willow thought. She looked at the creatures who were already trying to find a place under the tree for shade. Looking up at the sky the clouds swirled and a darkness fell over the area, but no rain fell. She apologized for not shading them earlier, when they first arrived.

The Hannulate were impressed by the human girl's actions. She showed respect and great strength. They agreed to return to their homeland if she would come through and help rebuild a place were they could live. Faramund once again summoned his transportation powers to move himself and a creature who identified itself as Shakine to the location of the other team, where they approached Aslo before confronting the other Hannulate with news of the agreement that had been made. In the end the whole process took less than thirty minutes before they returned to the portal location. They found Willow and the others at the stone base where the doorway between worlds would open.

Several more apple trees had already been created by the time they arrived, to feed their starving new friends and the creatures ate as if they had never seen food before.

"Those teeth and claws for...eating fruit?" Mike mused.

"More of a defensive tool they developed to escape captivity. They are naturally a peaceful race," Willow answered. She moved forward to the portal base and looked at the stones which were still embedded in the corners, the same as the one in her home land. She knew exactly what to do.

"Stand back, this is going to take some electricity," she yelled so that everyone could hear. Holding her palms face up, she looked directly into the sky above. A gold dust appeared from her hands and swirled up as if caught in a mini tornado high to the clouds. A darkness fell over the area and a rumble turned into a loud boom of thunder. Rain fell over the stone base and a bright flash as a single bolt of lightening struck the stone base releasing the corner stones which sprung into the air forming four corners of a door with a glowing light show of colours in between them.

Willow smiled and turned to Shakine. "Your doorway home." She bowed.

"We would ask for you to go through the portal first, as we agreed," it hissed back.

Willow took a step towards the open portal, when Mike grabbed her arm and pulled her back. "You can't actually be serious about going through. There is a good chance something horrible is waiting for you. Keepers are a hot target."

"I gave my word and I will help them rebuild their home. You can't expect them to return there to await certain death with no water sources or food," she answered pulling her arm away. She had barely begun moving towards the portal again when she was almost knocked over.

"I will go first," Mike said pushing in front of her through the doorway.

Willow sighed, following his lead and disappearing into the lights.

Stepping off the stone base a wave of heat hit Willow's face. She took a moment to look around at the surroundings. The land was as she had been told, barren. The earth appeared as a golden sand that had been stripped of all nutrients which could sustain plant life. There were what was left of trees, now dead, similar to that which might be found in the darkest nightmare. The ground around them was scattered with dead yellow tall grasses. The Hannulate who remained were huddled under make shift roofs constructed from dead leaves, wood and grass. They looked weak most likely from lack of food and water. Mike stood beside her taking in the same sights, Shakine and the others were behind them.

"You better be a real magic worker to fix all this," Mike said.

"Best get to work."

Willow took a deep breath and let it out slowly, then knelt down, picking up handfuls of dirt and let the soil pour between her fingers like sand in an hour glass. Moving to a second spot she did the same again, except instead of letting it fall, she took a deep breath and blew the dirt from her hands. Grains of soil flew through the air with only a few granules falling at a time. As they touched the ground, the colour of the earth changed to a deep brown earth colour, rich and moist. She stood, looking at the ground she had just healed as sprouts of life began appearing at equal intervals. Within minutes an orchard of fully grown apple trees with ripe fruit was standing before her. Looking to the skies she asked the clouds to form and provide cover from the sun.

The creatures who had just returned helped their friends and family over to the living trees so that they could eat and regain their energy. Shakine moved to Willow's side.

"Can you show me where the water pools were before?" she asked.

"There to the north and one larger to the east. There were rivers that flowed between, with dense forest land around," it answered pointing to spots.

"And what other types of fruit or vegetables would you like for your food source? Are there any plants that are dangerous to your kind that I should not create?"

The Hannulate listed off preferred foods, as well as those which must not be included and Willow began her work. There world was about twice the size of what her own had been and it would take her a while to complete the necessary changes to allow it to sustain life on its own again.

Her first task was to create large storms over where the two main bodies of water used to be located. The water would take several hours to pool back up to levels that were previously available. This was an unusual request for her, as her homeland had no such water reserves, but as promised she complied with the Hannulate requests.

Taking more handfuls of sand she turned her attention to rebuilding the nutrients in the dirt allowing it to sustain life once again. She blew the soil granules once again, but this time a gust of wind picked them up and moved it over larger areas. She continued replenishing the earth until all of the world's ground hand been transformed.

Willow touched the dirt and like a wave, a lush green grass grew covering all open areas of ground. Trees grew in orchards of peaches, plums, cherries, pears and oranges. Vines grew with grapes and assorted berries. Wild patches of pumpkins, squash and melons appeared as well as patches of tomatoes and legumes. Moving towards the smaller lake of water she turned her attention to the river creating a line of rain clouds connecting through to the larger sea. Along the river beds lush green forests grew with beautiful flowers of all colours and sizes, that would bloom continuously and glow at night, reminding her of the castle gardens from her home.

Willow had expended an enormous amount of energy and took a moment to relax under an apple tree beside Mike. Together they shared an apple.

"I have to say you didn't do too bad squirt," he smiled.

She was about to reply when several Hannulate approached them.

"You have created a beautiful world for us. We give you our thanks," Shakine said. "There is something we must show you that we believe you may have interest in. It was left here by the ones who brought the destruction."

One of the creatures moved forward and was holding something in its hands. It was very small, black and motionless.

"Is that...a bird?" Mike asked.

"It is an Allaren, one of the avian guardians," Willow said moving closer to see the mutilated body. "What did they do to the poor thing?"

"Torture comes in many forms. For those who can beg for death there is escape, but for the immortal, it can continue until the mind breaks as bad as the body. This Allaren is broken. We fear it may never recover, but perhaps you can bring it to a more comfortable place for it to spend eternity," Shakine said with sincerity.

Willow reached her hands out and took the motionless body. Silently she stroked the bird very gently not wanting to cause an additional pain. She could see from a basic glance over a wing had been removed, bones were broken, including its neck, its eyes were missing along with much of its feathers.

"What are you doing?" Mike asked.

"I need to bring her back with us," Willow said as she looked up at him her eyes watering. Placing her hand on the bird's head she barely heard Aslo and Kiera's voices pleading her to be careful. There was no going back, she was asking the motionless guardian to join with her so she could transport it back to the main world. The bird began to transform into a sparkling dust that looked like thousands of tiny diamond specks floating in the air flowing towards her left forearm where a picture began to form. It was an exact picture of the black bird as it had appeared including all of the injuries.

Willow turned to Mike. "I have to get back now." She was holding her stomach, the colour quickly fading from her face.

Mike wasted no time he picked her up and ran through the portal. Appearing on the other side he yelled for help. Willow was fading in and out of reality, drifting into an unconscious state.

Chapter Nineteen

The world was swirling around...images...colours...lights...voices. Peering left and right, there was nothing familiar. Her reality was distorted, then blackness. When she opened her eyes she was somewhere else...somewhere she hadn't been before. Visions surrounded her in all directions, dancing pictures on a circular screen, like a broken movie, flashing an immortal lifetime of experiences, jumping from one to another. The images began speeding up. She spun around in circles trying to keep up but it was moving too fast. The pictures appeared and disappeared before she knew what they were as if whoever was playing the movie was looking for a particular scene.

'*Of course,*' she thought. '*It's you. Your mind must be injured and this is the only way you can communicate with me. Aslo, Kiera, the others they aren't with us. They must have escaped, good. Well, I am not awake and I know you can't communicate with me in dreams so I am not asleep. Guess that means I am somewhere in between. So, what is it you are trying to show me my new friend?*'

There was no indication of how long she had been in this state, watching random pictures moving so fast that she didn't have time to make sense of shapes or voices, then to her surprise, the pictures began to slow. It was some sort of a fight. There was a woman she recognized, but wasn't exactly sure where from. The woman had strawberry coloured hair, much lighter than Willow's but with the same curls. A large bang sounded. Willow covered her ears as she watched the woman's body tumble to the ground, where she lay without movement. A group of men surrounded her. Willow recognized the uniforms they were wearing as the same as the men wore who attacked her home just days ago. They took the woman through a hole in the fabric of space into another world. Everything went dark.

Willow could hear voices, at first it was mumbled, but then they became clearer. It was a familiar voice. One from the day when the attack on her home world had first happened. It was the first man who had come through the rip between worlds and caused the destruction.

"Your keeper is injured and we will kill her...unless you surrender yourself to us. We know your partner is still joined with the woman. It would be terrible if he was also lost. Of course you could remain here, but we both know, with no keeper you would be locked here alone. There would be no way for you to leave and nothing to do but think about how you let your family die. Choose well. You have ten minutes."

Willow could feel exactly what her guest guardian had felt, the indecision, the guilt, the pain and the final surrender. She realized she was seeing, hearing and feeling everything the injured guardian had. The way it had. She was witnessing history as a part of it.

The vision shifted to another world. They were moving quickly now. It was no longer a picture, but rather Willow was the bird, as if she was there in its place. She was restrained in some way. It felt like heavy chains although she couldn't see them. The skies and the ground looked as if they were on fire and the seas were shiny black. They passed several small towns before coming to a forest, the plants and trees all looked dead, but were moving, as if sensing their presence. She shivered, the hairs on the back of her neck standing at attention.

The men transporting walked in single formation on the road as if scared to come too close to the forest edge, until they ran into a man going in the other direction. From his appearance, Willow deducted he was some sort of worker. His clothes were dirty and ripped. Signs of age showed on his face and fear was painted as a picture in his eyes. He lowered his line of sight, bowing his head down, so not to make eye contact with the officers in front of the procession, but they were not willing to share the road. The men stopped, knocking the worker to the side. A large vine grabbed the old man and pulled him in wrapping around him as if tying him to the trunk of the tree. Willow clenched her eyes closed tightly at the horrific sight. The bark started to engulf him, bit by bit. The tree was eating him alive. The man screamed for help, pain resonating in his voice, as the soldiers just stood and laughed. Then silence and the old man was gone. The group started walking again as if nothing had happened.

At the end of the forest was a mountain of black rock with a single smooth road carved in a circular motion. Along the way to the top they passed several plateaus. One resembled a market place with items for everyday use, probably where the old man had been, the others looked like army barracks. At the top was a grand entrance way to what looked like a castle, built out of the same rock as the mountain.

The stone doors were open and people inside were cheering, celebrating, welcoming them. She could hear echos of '*good job*', '*well done sir*' and '*caught another one, brilliant isn't he*'. The group stopped before a man and woman who dressed as if they felt themselves important, in fine silk clothes of bright colours, adorned with animal furs. Both wore excessive amounts of jewels. The man stepped forward.

"Well done my son, well done indeed. Another filthy creature." He turned to the others standing around in admiration. "A toast to my son!" He lifted his cup. "We protect the worlds from oppression and confinement. This beast took away our freedom and now we take away the same from it, so it can no longer impose its will on innocent people." The man drank.

The room broke out in a chorus of, "Hail, King Cornelius! Long live the king." Then Willow was moving again to a set of winding stone stairs. She lost count of how many levels they went down leading her to conclude they must be inside the mountain. At the very bottom were what appeared to be rooms, but made out of some sort of glass on one side and rock on the other. She could see inside the rooms, each housing guardians and keepers, all injured worn, tired and sad. In one room she saw the strawberry haired lady.

"You said you would let them go if I surrendered, honour the agreement prince." Willow found she was saying the words as if scripted.

"No, you are mistaken." The prince laughed. "I said I wouldn't kill them and I won't. Anything else is fair game."

"We have done you no harm. Let them go," she pleaded.

"No harm? No harm? You destroyed our world, our people. You tried to oppress us. You deviated from the true path of a guardian. You chose to impose your will on others by forcing them into worlds of your choice. If it weren't for Apopp and his kind you may have gotten away with it. They will help us regain our dignity and rights," he said then turned to an empty cell. "Put it in there and if it gives you any trouble hurt it and its keeper."

He disappeared back up the steps. Willow was cold, sad, afraid, so many emotions were running through her at once. Every so often a few guards would enter and accuse her of plotting something then hit her with sticks which gave off bolts of energy. Welts formed on her skin from the abuse. Gasping for air, her eyes stung until tears flowed freely down the sides of her face. Hours faded to days and time passed, the guards continued their attacks daily but there was enough time between for her to heal herself. Then something changed.

The prince returned. "We need some information. My father Cornelius would like his sister returned. She was taken from us when the division occurred. If you can tell us where she is...well we can be lenient on you and the woman."

Willow found herself speaking the bird's words again. "Even if I knew who you were speaking of I would not tell you. No creature deserves the daily torture you inflict."

"She is my Aunt. Why would I hurt her?" Joseph asked pacing.

"Jealousy, prejudice...I am not sure why you torture any of us or how any person could be so cold as to gain pleasure by inflicting physical pain on others."

The Prince stormed out of the room slamming the door behind him. There was no question...she had enraged him. A shiver ran down her spine, knowing she would pay a price for refusing to answer his questions. He returned a few minutes later with several men and a case of tools.

"Wrong answer, perhaps your keeper will speak to save you," he said smiling. "Since you don't want to talk, maybe you shouldn't be able to."

The men secured her with chains to a rock wall as Joseph removed knives and pliers from the case. Within seconds Willow could only feel pain, so severe she couldn't see. It was everywhere there was nothing else just pain. She begged for it to stop. She didn't know how long she could continue to live with this torture, it felt like cycles had past of continuous pain. Her mind began shutting down unable to handle anymore.

Chapter Twenty

"Quickly, move her to the infirmary." William motioned to Mike to bring Willow's limp body to a bed where they could give her medical attention. Searching the camp they needed to find both Victoria and conventional medical help. Returning with their on site doctor and nurse, they were greeted by thirteen black cats.

"What has happened? Why have you separated from her?" William asked his eyes bulging.

"We can help more from here. She is weak. We don't know what is going to happen. Right now she is neither awake nor asleep, and comfortable, but soon she could feel all the guardian bird experienced, and share in it. Such torture is too much for anyone to endure," Aslo answered. "If her body shows signs of pain or stress she needs to be sedated. We must ensure she is asleep, it is the only way to break the telepathic connection between them."

The door flung open and Victoria ran in followed by her three brothers. Without speaking the young girl ran to the bed side and placed her hands on Willow's arm. Silence fell over the room, no one wanting to disturb the healer's concentration. After several minutes Victoria turned around looked at her brothers and shook her head. Tears formed in the young girl's eyes. Jessie stepped forward putting his arms around his sister just in time. She burst into sobs. Everyone knew there was nothing she could do. Willow's health now rested in the hands of the human medical team which consisted of a young husband and wife, Richard and Mary.

The doctor and nurse proceeded to hook up machines and wires to monitor the patient, took scans and ran tests. It would be hours before any news would be available. Aslo and his family insisted on staying to watch over their keeper, while the others returned to the main house to tell the rest of the camp what had happened.

It would take the next hour for William to try to explain to the others in the command centre the events that had occurred as best as he could. There was mood was solemn and the air went stale. Everyone tried to come up with ideas on how to heal the young girl lying in the medical building. Not knowing what could be done was ominous. So many questions were raised.

"How did she manage to bond with an avian guardian when she is a feline guardian keeper?" Diana asked. "That has never done before. I thought cross guardian race bonding was not possible."

"There are a lot of things we don't yet understand," William answered. "How could she carry not just more than two guardians but fourteen? No keeper had ever been able to heal their counter part before. How will she do that?" He rubbed the back of his neck. "There are harder questions to ask as well. How could she escape from a broken mind? What will her mind be like if she does wake? Will she carry the same scars as the guardian she is trying to heal?" He paused for a moment. "We just don't know the answers."

Mike noticed a boy sitting alone at the table in the corner. He was looking at various books, but never seemed to open any and didn't appear to be concerned at all. He nudged William and motioned in that direction. Everyone turned to look at the boy.

"Nathan," Diana said. "Are you alright? I know you and Willow were close."

"Yes Gran I am fine, and she will be too," he answered. "It's in the book."

"Which book? What do you mean?" Mike asked.

"*The Portal Prophecies*," Nathan answered. "Prophecy number twenty-three, although I don't think they are in any particular order."

Diana walked over and picked up he book she rubbed the cover as if for luck and then opened it flipping the pages to the exact prediction her grandson had spoken of and read it out loud.

> *' A race forgotten shall appear again, in need of intervention*
>
> *one soul so pure shall see the cause and alter what could be,*
>
> *devastation averted, a world now saved,*
>
> *one life shall be the reward, within it's mind a soul has been lost*
>
> *and another shall fall to slumber, the signs on doors to show the way,*
>
> *with rest and time life shall renew and mind shall mend*
>
> *all shall emerge with questions answered*
>
> *life preserved and new hope granted.'*

"Once you figure out the wording you can see it applies to what happened today. Problem is figuring out what they all mean before they come true. That might be difficult. It is something we should work on though. Some of the stuff in there sounds pretty bad so if we could avoid them happening it would be beneficial," Nathan said.

"Problem with prophecies are the future isn't set in stone. They guide you as to what could happen, but we don't know if something we do causes them to happen or stops it. Not an exact science," Clairity said chewing on her finger nail.

"The ones who wrote this book felt these particular predictions would be something needed in the future. They were insistent that I record them for them. No explanations, just that one day it would be important. They are the only prophecies our world ever recorded," Diana added.

"You didn't ask what they meant?" Mike asked.

"No, it was before the war. I was just a book maker. It was my job. There was no reason for me to ask." Diana rubbed her arms as if she were cold, although there was no chill in the house and a fire was raging in the fireplace.

William flipped through the book. "There are a lot of prophecies in here. Do we know if any of them have happened already? Ones that we can...cross off the list?"

"We know the one about leaving our home world happened. It's how we got here. Willow deciphered it." Diana took the book and flipped the pages again then read out loud the passage.

"When the blue flames engulf the land,

only one whose will is steadied by that discovered

can break that which is set in stone to escape."

She handed the large book back to the guard, who examined the page. "From that she figured out how to open a portal?" he asked.

"No, there were other things too, like our dreams. They were about the last minutes on our world. Everything was the same except in the dreams, there was a massive storm over the forest...and I think she mentioned another prophecy. I don't know where she heard about it, but it was about her. Something about being different from birth and needing to figure things out for herself." Ashlyn had been withdrawn through the whole meeting, as if thinking. "Maybe I could contact her. If she is asleep I mean, in her dreams...make sure she is okay."

"We aren't sure she is asleep at the moment. If we sedate her...it's an option we are willing to discuss." William looked around the room for any reaction from the others.

"Is that dangerous?" Diana asked.

"We don't know, but we do know if she seems in pain we will have to induce sleep to calm her."

"You should make her sleep, the prophecy says so. It is the only way!" Nathan exclaimed not believing they were discussing this. He headed for the door.

"Slow down dude," Mike said grabbing the boy. "The doctor is running some tests first. We will have the results soon. Aslo and Kiera are watching her. If she looks stressed they will make sure she is sedated. Okay?"

Nathan nodded and sat down again.

"So Nathan, Diana...you two should head up a team to try and figure out some of the prophecies. Look for patterns, or indications of something that could be happening at the moment or in the near future first. There are too many to do every single one at once. Eventually we will need to know them all though. Pick a team to help you...and call a meeting when you have anything to brief us all. Sarah, you continue working on the maps and location of missing stones for portals. I would sleep a lot better if we had them in our possession. Work in shifts so everyone gets some rest and we have fresh eyes. Anyone not on a team please head to bed, tomorrow we start training for your abilities and self defence." William rubbed the stubble growing on his face. It had been a couple days since he had any time to shave. Looking around the room he could see several of the other men were in the same position. It's definitely going to be a long haul this time he thought to himself.

He motioned to Ashlyn and Mike to join him and the three headed back over to the medical centre. There had been no change in Willow's condition and the test results weren't back yet. Suddenly her body began to shake and twitch. Aslo jumped up, eyes widened and focused on the red headed girl.

"She is in pain," the guardian said. "She needs sedation now. There is no time to wait for test results. You have to trust me. She must sleep."

The medical team had seen enough strange things happen in their time at the camp, that they knew better than to argue with a talking cat, who might one day be the only thing standing between their world as it is and complete destruction. They prepared a sedative to make Willow sleep.

Ashlyn laid down in the bed beside her friend. "Could I have a light sedative so I can try to reach Willow in her dreams?" she asked.

Ashlyn had only discovered in the past few weeks she had the gift of dream walker and was still experimenting with what that meant. She knew she could call someone close to her into her dreams if she was emotional, especially scared, although so far she had only contacted her mother. Willow had been able to call her for help once as well. They had shared the same dream, a foretelling of the devastation of their home world. She wasn't exactly sure if she could enter her friend's dreams or not yet. This would be a completely new experience, but she had to try.

Mary handed a tiny white pill to Ashlyn. "This will only help you fall asleep. You will be able to wake up if necessary within a couple of hours."

Richard had already given some form of medication to Willow through what he called a needle. Ashlyn heard them say her heart rate and blood pressure was already returning to normal levels and she showed no more signs of pain or stress. *'Time to go in,'* Ashlyn thought to herself as she swallowed the pill, her body flopping back on the bed. She was worried her nervousness might hinder her ability to sleep and was considering other ways to help relax enough to drift off. When she opened her eyes everything was white for as far as she could see.

She was asleep. Now to find Willow. She called to her a few times concentrating as hard as she could on her friend, how she looked, how she talked. Looking around, the room was white, the walls were white, her dress was white. She mused at how her hair had just chosen its final colour in the last two weeks and it too was white, although with pastel pink streaks. It was perfectly straight and hung down just above her shoulders, except for bangs which covered her forehead. She was happy that it no longer changed colour with her moods as was the case with all the girls under sixteen cycles from her homeland. Her hair colour now highlighted her facial features perfectly. She was petite with grey eyes so light they were almost silver colour, a small nose, perfectly pink cheeks and small red lips.

Walking forward, she noticed up ahead closed doors were forming before her eyes, hundreds of them. She began turning knobs, but every one she tried was locked. Frustration set in. She ran frantically from door to door trying to find one she could open, but none would. After about thirty doors, she stopped. Bending over at the waist, she gasped for air. Slowly her red flushed face returned to normal and her heart rate slowed. *'Now what?'* she asked herself knowing there would be no answer. She was at a loss. How was she supposed to know which door led to her friend? Her small framed body slid to the ground and she pulled her knees to her chest. She sighed. Tilting her head upwards, something caught her attention. Getting up, she moved close to the door in front of her. There on the knob was a green gem, a jade. The prophecy had told her what to do.

Of course she thought, each door had a sign on them as to who was behind the door. Something that spoke to her, that she could understand. There would be a door for everyone she knew who was currently sleeping. Unfortunately that was most of the camp, so she would have a lot of doors to examine to find the one that led to Willow.

After examining several doors, she came across one with a black bird on the handle. *'I wonder,'* she thought, *'maybe'*...she turned the door knob and it opened. Stepping through Ashlyn found herself in another white room with a single door in it. On the floor was a black bird.

"Are you trying to go through there?" Ashlyn asked.

"I can't. Someone has to open the door and let me through," the bird answered. "It's the door you are looking for. You can help her. Don't leave her alone, she needs someone to protect her."

She moved closer to the door and examined the symbols on the handle. They were changing so fast she couldn't make out what any of them were.

"What does this mean?" she asked pointing to the signs.

"The girl is someone to whom everything and nothing applies. She chooses her own path and then can create it. A strength which until now has never been seen. It is unclear how far she can stretch the reality the rest of us are bound to."

Ashlyn reached for the handle and was shocked when it turned easily. She opened it slowly and turned back to the bird still standing behind her as if she wanted to ask a question.

"She isn't ready to see me yet. I am here if you need anything. She will need to talk to you about things she has seen...felt. She needs a friend she already knows."

Ashlyn walked through closing the door behind her. The room she entered was still white without any furniture or anything, except sitting in the middle was Willow, wearing a similar white dress, which made her deep red curly hair stand out and her skin tone look very tanned.

"Willow!"

The girl in the middle of the room looked up at her with relief written all over her face. "How did you find me?"

"Getting better at this I guess." Ashlyn smiled. "Are you okay?"

"I saw them...the ones who destroyed our home...they were the same ones who hurt the guardian bird." the colour quickly disappeared from Willow's face as she thought back to the images she had seen. "I saw their home world, where the others are being held. They have our people and guardians locked up in rooms. They hurt them, torture them. We have to save them." Her mind wandered to the boy named Lance. She hadn't seen him there but she knew he was a part of that world.

"How? They have an army Willow. We aren't strong enough."

"I don't know yet, but there has to be a way. We can't leave them and that will be where they took the survivors from the attack on or home land as well."

"Did you see them?" Ashlyn asked.

"No, what I saw happened before that. It was what the bird saw and felt. The torture that was inflicted on the poor thing. I thought I was going to die from the pain."

"I think you almost did. Richard the doctor gave you a sedative so you would sleep. Aslo said that would help you."

"Ohhhh." A smile came over Willow's face. "Of course they can't enter my dreams. But, I can't stay asleep forever."

"I know we are working on it." Ashlyn thought about telling her friend about what was outside the door she had come through, but decided it was better to wait.

"Did you feel that?" Willow asked standing up to look around.

"Feel what?" Ashlyn began to answer when the room shook like they were in a mini earthquake. "Whoa!" She said putting her arms out to catch her balance.

The room shook again this time harder. The room started to change. There was a fireplace and comfortable chairs with a tapestry type rug on the floor. The changes were coming closer and the white room was disappearing. Then appeared a boy. He had blue black hair with bangs that hung down over his piercing blue eyes and he dressed all in black. He smiled at Ashlyn and said, "Sorry private party," while waving.

Ashlyn felt her body propelling backwards. The door opened, throwing her out before slamming behind her. She could hear Willow scream. Looking up she saw she was on the floor and the bird was looking over her.

"Are you okay? The girl?" it asked her.

"I don't know," Ashlyn described what had happened during the visit.

"Lance...the boy you described, one of the princes in the world that we are fighting. This is dangerous. You need to open the door again and help her."

"I can't, he knew I was there. He won't let me back in." Salty tears cascaded down her pale face kissing her lips.

"Then let me in," the bird yelled.

Ashlyn looked at it. "I can do that? How?"

"You can do more than you know child, you just haven't tried. This world belongs to you, with practice you can do anything."

"So the boy, Lance...he is a dream walker too? That is how he made the room?"

"Yes, their whole family has the gift and they have had many years practice," the bird said. "Just open the door and tell it you are allowing me to enter."

Chapter Twenty-One

Everything was happening so quickly. One minute Willow was talking to her friend Ashlyn and now here she was standing in a lavish room face to face with the boy from the forest. His piercing blue eyes were staring straight into hers, as if seeing her soul.

"Hello," he said with a smile. "I was wondering if we would ever meet again. Tell me how did you escape the necrid fire?"

"How...how did you get into my dream? What happened to my friend?" Willow barked.

"How?" he laughed. "You called me here. Actually, seems a little unfair you know my name and I don't know yours."

Willow realized earlier she had thought of him for a brief moment. "Lance...your name. I was thinking of the forest and what happened. That was enough to call you here?"

"Yes, but how exactly do you know my name?" Lance moved to the back of a chair and rested against it waiting for a reply.

"I heard someone call you in the forest when I was running away," she said.

"So, back to the beginning, You know my name, but what is yours?" he said.

"Why did you do it? Why did you destroy my home?" Willow asked ignoring the prince's question.

"That is a long story. Why don't you tell me how you escaped?" he asked getting a bit aggravated.

That seemed to be an ongoing theme for her with boys, she aggravated them. Willow's mind turned to a similar conversation she had with Mike. She decided after remembering the duct tape that she needed to come up with an answer for the prince.

"I...don't know," she answered with a sigh. "I know I was in an accident and a doctor sedated me so I could rest. If you had let my friend stay longer she might have told me more." She wasn't really lying about that, so even if he had the ability to sense an untruth he wouldn't question what she had just said. She wasn't about to give him more information than she needed to. He may be cute but she wasn't stupid.

"So, where are you?" he asked.

"I...don't know." Again she wasn't lying, she never asked where exactly she was. Thinking back she realized how odd that was, and she also didn't know where her body was either maybe a medical facility of some sort, maybe a room or maybe lying in a field.

"You don't know anything?" he mused.

"My friend...she was trying to see if I was okay. That's why she was here to contact me." This all not only sounded true it was all true.

"That sucks." He moved around and sat in a chair by the fire.

"Your turn," Willow said moving closer. "Why did you do it?"

"I told you it's a long story."

"I have no where to go," she answered.

"Okay, well a long time ago there were six ancient races, the serpents, the spiders, the sea creatures, the cats, the birds and a dog type animal. They monitored the world and called themselves guardians. The guardians had...powers, abilities stronger than any other creature alive. They watched over things but their policy was not to get involved in the world, to let other beings live out their lives without influence."

"Three of races felt things weren't being handled correctly. They split off and decided that to keep things the way they wanted. They confined all worlds, separate from each other, especially locking in serpents, spiders and sea creatures in different worlds...to ensure their way would not be challenged. They kidnapped people from the stronger realms thinking that would stop any uprisings."

"The serpents, were the original sleep walkers and contacted different leaders among men, to find one who could help them stop the oppression which was being forced on us all. They chose my father. Together they began working on a way to make the walls between worlds disappear. At first just a small hole was all that could be managed. Knowing how much time it was going to take to complete the task the serpent leader Apopp sent through a chalice of his venom for the King and Queen, my parents, to drink. It granted them and their family line new abilities and extended life. Now we can create an opening for long enough to enter and search worlds for the rogue guardians and make sure they have no where to hide. Our goal is to eradicate them, break down the walls that were put up and ultimately protect all beings from them."

Willow couldn't believe what she was hearing. "You actually believe that?" she shrieked without thinking. She could see anger building in his eyes that she was questioning him, but she couldn't stop. "It doesn't make any sense."

"Really," he answered. "What doesn't make sense?"

"You say your goal is to save people from oppression and destruction. Yet you enter worlds uninvited, kill or imprison the people, force them to join your army and do what you want, then you destroy everything in their home land."

"It's the only way to find them, to imprison the ancients that are still hiding, to ensure they don't stand in our way or destroy any other families." He yelled loud enough to make her stumble backwards.

She caught her balance. "How many families are you destroying doing this? How many in my world did you kill or take away? How do you even know these serpents are telling you the truth? How do you know what you are doing is right? What gives you the right to decide?"

"We are putting right an injustice that was done to us and all other creatures...We were the victims, imprisoned in a small world to ensure we could not progress further and challenge for power."

"You're the victims?" Willow yelled. "You kill parents and children and take away free will from others for what? To ensure your world advances in power? To help a bunch of snakes take over all existence? Just because you feel you were wronged doesn't give you the right to wrong others or take life away from anyone or anything."

"My father was there. He saw what they did, lives were lost. My Aunt Diana was taken by them as their prisoner. If it were you wouldn't you want your family back? My father longs for the day he will see his beloved sister again."

Willow snorted. "Yeah, it is me. I want my family back. I guess I need a hero world to go get them back for me and kill my oppressors. Oh, sorry that would be you."

"You don't understand." Lance said his hands forming fists.

Willow interrupted. "Yes I do. You are doing exactly what you say was done to you, except to other worlds and then justifying your actions by saying you are stopping it from happening again." She was angry now and clear thought wasn't an option. "And when I get out of here I am going to find my friends and family and set them free. I will spend my lifetime making sure you and your sick family never hurt anyone ever again."

"You stupid girl," he said grabbing her arm hard. "Do you think you can challenge an empire? What is to stop me from killing you right now? Do you know what happens when you die in your sleep? You die in real life too, our minds can't distinguish between that sort of trauma."

She broke free from his grasp and slapped him, but he was more amused than hurt by it. His eyes were laughing at her. Still through all this there was something about the boy that excited her. He was dangerous and made her feel free, alive.

The room shook and both of them stumbled backwards. The scenery was changing again, within moments they were standing on a field surrounded by forests. Looking up there was what looked like a large bird circling over them.

"That's...impossible," Lance said.

"What is it?" Willow asked. It was unlike anything she had ever seen. Its wing span alone must have been three or four times the size of the largest man she knew. It was gliding majestically above them circling as if searching for prey, yet she didn't feel afraid, but she could tell Lance was. The young prince took a few steps backwards and the bird landed between the two of them.

"I recognize that scar. How did you get here...your mind was broken."

"It has been healed," the bird answered. "And I was let in by someone who cares for this girl. Now it is time for you to go." The bird opened its wings and flapped them creating a wind that blew the boy back through the doorway he had entered through. The door slammed behind him and he was gone.

"Are you alright?" the bird asked.

Willow was still unsure. "Yes," she answered, "but who are you...are you the guardian I helped?"

"Yes, my name is Shelby. I owe you a great debt. It is an honour to meet the one the prophecies spoke of."

"You know of the prophecies?" Willow asked.

"Yes, sight is an ability of all avian guardians which we can extend to the person we are joined with. For the clairvoyant it enhances their powers. That is how many prophecies came to be, which meant at least one of us was present and experienced predictions as they happened. There was also one visionary named Iris, she shared her predictions, what she saw, with my keeper. They were the ones who decided to record the book, '*The Portal Prophecies*'."

"So you could tell us what some of them mean?"

"No," Shelby seemed to laugh. "The interpretation of the words of a prophecy are important. They can mean one thing to you and apply, but they can mean another to someone else and also apply. While you are the one spoken of in some prophecies, they do not all have a message for you. It is important you understand that. There are others who must contribute to your goals as well. You are not alone nor are you meant to be alone."

"What about what happened to you? Will there be a time when I can safely wake up? Is there something I can do to help you?" Willow asked.

"You have already done all that you can, I am healing, it won't be long now. You are a brave girl with a real talent for bending rules. Thank you for saving me. Now we must rest, think of no one my friend, just sleep."

Chapter Twenty-Two

Ashlyn sat up instantly as if she had never been asleep or sedated. She had no idea how long she had been in the dream world. Time there was much different from real life. Minutes there could be hours awake and vice versa. Looking around she could see it wasn't morning yet and to her surprise Mike was asleep on an extra bed. She figured it had to be some macho protection thing he came up with, to keep the sleeping beauties safe. The thought made her chuckle a little. Then she looked over at her friend and wondered what was happening. Had the bird been able to help or was Willow trapped with that boy?

Walking over, she looked at the picture on the sleeping girl's arm. The bird looked different. It wasn't as mangled anymore. It was healthier, healing. But would Willow be safe until it healed completely? Could people be hurt and die in a dream? She didn't know the answers but figured she had better wake Mike and get the others together to discuss what she had discovered and decide where to go from here.

Ashlyn learnt quickly waking Mike from a sound sleep could be dangerous. He had grabbed her and almost hit her before he realized there wasn't a threat. For the first time she wondered what had happened to him. She had heard stories from the others as to their experiences with unusual creatures and how it affected them. Something horrible must have been in Mike's past she thought, something that made him so subconsciously aware of his surroundings that he could perceive a threat.

Mike released his grip and apologized. Ashlyn quickly told him she had important information and needed to gather everyone to go over it.

"It can't wait till morning, a couple more hours? Everyone will be tired," Mike said yawning.

"No," she insisted. "It can't wait, Willow may still be in danger as well as others."

"Others?" Mike seemed a bit confused. "Okay, I will wake the troops. We can meet in the command centre." He walked out brushing his short hair with his hand heading towards the building William was sleeping in.

Ashlyn sat for a moment on the edge of Willow's bed and whispered, "Hang in there," to her, then added, "both of you," looking at the picture of the black bird on her arm. For a moment she thought she saw it wink at her, maybe because it had eyes again she thought, or the light was playing tricks with hers. She smiled out of the corner of her mouth and headed over to the command centre.

To her surprise the main room of the house was already bustling with activity. The prophecy team was busy at work, two people would sleep in the back bedroom or on the couch, while the others read and tried to decipher meanings from the ancient text. It wasn't going so well from what Ashlyn could tell, but at least she had good news. Nathan had been right, the prophecy they discussed yesterday had been about Willow sleeping, but there had also been a message to her as well. It told her to follow the signs on the doors. That was what led her to Willow.

Behind her the door opened, the others were filing in, some yawning, some still in night clothes. She was particularly amused by the fuzzy pink bunny slippers Sarah was wearing. It was such a contrast from her usual orderly appearance she had grown accustomed to over the past days. Ashlyn wasn't the only one who noticed. Mike was already teasing her and Sarah's face turned numerous shades of red. Little giggles exploded all over the room.

In the corner, Zsiga was standing at the coffee maker. It had fascinated him since he first was shown what it was used for. Since then he had insisted on making fresh pots of coffee every time he was in the command centre. The first few pots were less than desirable and the others, to be nice, pretended to drink them, then suggested he use a little less coffee next time, throwing it out when he left. Now, he wasn't too bad. The smell of fresh coffee was filling the air louring several people who were half-asleep, following the aroma with mugs in hand waiting for a cup of instant wake up.

The three portal guards had all been interested with the technology of this world. They had never been exposed to anything even slightly like the devices and machines they were finding here and had been spending all their free time learning about how different things functioned.

William stood in front of the large map board by the fireplace. He called for the attention of everyone. Once the last few had found a seat, the guardians, Aslo, Kiera and their family were lying comfortably by the fire in their house cat forms and everyone looked ready, he motioned for Ashlyn to come to the front of the room and tell them what she had learnt.

She began to explain the story of her night with the prophecy and it's hidden meaning for her. The deciphering team was very interested in the information. This meant that every prophecy could mean several things to different people and perhaps needed multiple interpretations. Then Ashlyn told them about Willow, how she was, what she had experienced, and the images of the world where their friends and family were being held.

A slight grumble erupted at the thought that the young keeper might want to attack a world that had an army that could defeat large forces when they were so few.

"We should wait to disagree until she is here to tell us how and when," Ashlyn said. "But our friends...our family...if they are imprisoned and need help, I will stand by Willow and try to help them."

"I have a feeling there is more information somewhere, a prophecy or something we are missing that will tie everything together about who we are fighting and why. I think that will help us decide where we are heading," Clairity added. She had been Willow's best friend since birth basically and there was no question of where she would stand in a fight, not that she knew exactly how much help she would be. She knew her gift was sight, but she hadn't yet fully developed it. In fact she still just had *'feelings'* about things, that always rang true. The last few days she often thought that since heading into her sixteenth cycle the only thing she had developed was that her hair colour had settled on midnight black, the colour Willow had always said she liked the best.

"I did learn something else from the guardian bird," Ashlyn said. "Each of us still has a long way to go to discover what we can do, our abilities are as far as we choose to expand them and limitless. We all need practice."

"Agreed. We can begin training as soon as possible, today even. Unfortunately, we are limited to lessons we know or have been taught and from what I understand there wasn't much mentoring going on back home," William said.

"I can help with that," Malarchy offered, causing an uproar of whispers. "I know I made mistakes, but long ago I was an original council member and I helped set up classes to train people. I want to make up for my mistakes. I want to help. I want to see my son again." He began to weep. Everyone else was at a loss for words. Malarchy had never displayed any emotion to them before and now this, such sadness and regret, they almost felt sorry for him. Many not sure if they should feel contempt or pity for the man who was partly responsible for their world's destruction.

"Fine," William said. "You can work with Mike and pick some people to help you set up training later today. We need to advance the abilities of everyone, as well as learn hand to hand combat and weapon use. Now, what about our Willow? Where did you leave things with her?"

Ashlyn's face drained of colour as she retold the story of how she was kicked out of the dream by the boy and what the bird had told her about him. She explained that she let the guardian into her dream to protect her.

"That is what happened to me." Jade spoke for the first time since they had left her home. "Except it was Prince Joseph. He was supposed to take me away, just me. We were going to start a new life together. He was so caring, I believed him. I know that doesn't change what I did and I don't expect anyone to ever forgive me, nor will I ever forgive myself. I close my eyes and I see him killing my mother over and over." Her words faded off into sobs.

Neil snorted a '*Figures*' in the background, which everyone chose to ignore.

"Isn't that defeating the purpose? We sedated her to get away from the guardian," Mike asked, directing attention away from the obviously emotionally unstable girl and her disgruntled wannabe boyfriend.

It was Aslo that answered. "From what she has told us, I believe the Avian Guardian is healing and to the point where he or she can put what was experienced behind. It is most unusual. Until now it was thought a guardian needed to self heal if it was to heal at all. Did anyone happen to look at the picture on her arm to see if the image has changed at all?"

"Yes," Ashlyn answered. "The bird is much better looking. It has eyes and the wing has regrown."

"Then we need only worry about the boy. Bad things can still happen in dreams and if the mind believes them, some can be as real as if they were happening while awake," Aslo added.

"How do we help her then?" William asked.

"We trust that she is strong enough to get through it and that she has some help. Hopefully it wont be too long before she is awake again. I suggest we discontinue the sedatives," Kiera the other feline guardian answered this time. "Until then train as hard as you can. We will also help with development classes as needed."

"Okay, trainers pick your helpers and everyone I suggest we change, have something to eat and meet in the training field to discuss your abilities in a couple hours," William said ending the meeting.

Chapter Twenty-Three

It was a few hours before the training field was set up and ready to use. Much of the training would be based on physical skills and exploring uses of different physical talents. For those like Ashlyn, whose abilities could not be practised on a field, Mike had different forms of combat lessons available.

Mike had chosen Sarah, Iskander, Faramund and Zsiga to help him as well as a couple of other men from his world, to replace the portal guards while they trained their other skills on the field, if necessary. Malarchy had Aslo and Kiera as well as William and Diana on his team, trying to help advance magical skills.

First step was to explore what exactly everyone could do and figure out possible uses and advancement of their different talents.

Malarchy began with Ashlyn since she already had seen how her abilities could advance and things she could do in the future with training and hard work.

Ashlyn started by explaining what she had been able to do up until now and that her next steps were to locate people faster, change scenery, bring other people in and out of dreams and learn how to control the dream itself. This gave each of the others an idea of what they were trying to figure out about their own gifts.

Clairity offered to be next. "I have feelings, sometimes as to a place I should be or whether things are true or not. I think I should be working towards full prophecies and lie detection. I ironically enough, have a feeling there is also a physical aspect to my abilities I have not yet experienced, although I do not know what it is."

"Very good," Malarchy said. "The two of you would be good exercise partners, during the day work on simple mind reading in your extra time and at night work on dream walking and exploration. For now though, I think you both should join up with Mike and work on self defence basics. We have already seen the physical aspect of the attacks of our enemy and should be prepared for it."

Aslo and Kiera agreed and the two girls headed off to join Mike. Nathan was the next to step forward.

"Pretty much everyone knows I can read books without opening them and very quickly. I can also transfer the entire book to another person word for word with full comprehension. Since I am only twelve, I have four years to develop my gift. Probably, your time would be spent better on other people and I can continue working on the book of prophecies."

Diana smiled at how grown up her grandson had become over the past few weeks. She saw so much of his father in him and was proud. There was no doubt in anyone's mind that the boy needed to continue his work inside the command centre. With approval he headed back to his table and books.

Jessie stepped forward. "I have extra ordinary strength and speed. I would expect I need to develop how to use both at the same time. I may be able to move a large object, but if someone is attacking me I need to be able to evade them at the same time. I am not sure there will be anything other than brute force that I develop but I also think I will be proficient in most forms of combat naturally."

"Excellent, why don't you test that idea with Mike's team and see what happens," Aslo commented and the others agreed.

Pete stepped forward. "Things can't hit me," he said. "I mean like weapons, it's like I have an invisible shell around me. Not very exciting I am afraid."

Aslo moved close to the boy and examined him. "This is the best news we have heard. Your next step is to extend a shield to protect others and if I am correct one day you may be able to create containment fields and even enforce the barriers between the worlds which have grown thin. I will walk over with you to talk to Mike. I would like to see you trying to protect people against physical attacks."

Pete looked quite proud of himself as the two walked off to join the other team. He had always been the understudy to his two other brothers, the shortest, although still taller than most men, he was for lack of better description, the in between one, not really spectacular in any way, but now he was finally getting some recognition and stepping out from his brothers' shadows.

Malarchy motioned for Dezi to go next thinking the triplet brothers would stick together, but was surprised by his response.

"I don't know yet," Dezi said looking at the ground. It was unusual for him to shy away from anything and, even more curious, he was the only brother of the three that hadn't figured out what his ability was. "I think I should just work on combat for now." Without waiting for an answer, he headed over to the combat team and left everyone wondering what had just happened.

The next boy stepped forward and silence followed. Neil, everyone knew now as *'the boy who ripped open the space between worlds and let the invasion in'*. It wasn't his fault of course he had been bewitched by Jade into believing they were running away together to start a new life. He wasn't sure which was worse...being known as a weapon of destruction or a love struck pawn of Jade's.

"I can bend the reality of items," he said quietly. "I can rearrange the way they appear, their texture. I can change space. I am not sure after stretching the barrier between worlds thin enough to break if there is anything else I will advance to. It was terrible but still sort of epic."

"That it was," Malarchy answered. "That it was...but, there is always room for advancement. For instance you can change the way this rock looks and whether it is rough or smooth, but could you make it appear as a rock, but feel like a sponge? On a side note let's stay away from bending space and making holes for now and concentrate on something a little smaller. Perhaps Diana could work with you on that?"

Diana nodded and head off away from the crowd to work individually on Neil's talents, and keep an eye on what he was directing his attention to so no further *'accidents'* could happen.

Malarchy turned his attention to his daughter, the only remaining family member he had. "Jade, darling, can you tell us what your talents are?"

"Nothing worth anything," she said without looking up. She hadn't looked anyone in the face since the last day they were home. "I...can make myself look good, convince people to do what I want sometimes. That's it."

"Illusion can be a strong gift if you work on it. In one form or another, your mother and I have the same gift," Malarchy said.

"Had."

"Sorry dear?" he answered. The tone of his voice told everyone he had forgiven the girl for what had happened, or perhaps blamed himself. Either way she was his daughter and he loved her unconditionally, it didn't matter what she had done.

"Mother had that gift. She is dead now...and it's my fault. There is no illusion in that." Jade ran off back to the building in which she had been sleeping the past few days.

Victoria moved forward and tugged on Malarchy's sleeve. "I can practice healing anyone who gets hurt in practice combat if you like. I am still learning though and have a long way to sixteen."

"A wonderful idea. You head right over there and tell Uncle Mike you will be assisting with the wounded." He flashed a devious smile at Mike.

Victoria skipped away happy as could be to her new job. After a few looks from Mike for sending him the young girl to deal with for the day, Malarchy continued on. Looking over his list, Faramund had been excused to help with combat. They had already discussed his teleportation powers and practising with accuracy.

"Camile?" he said loudly.

"Potions," she replied. "I can make potions, for just about anything. Right now I use known potion recipes. The next step for me is to work on making my own up using ingredients readily available."

"Good, perhaps we should stay away from consumption ones for the time being and stick to ones that you pour on objects," Malarchy said, thinking back to the love potion she had created that had almost killed Jessie, Dezi and Pete. "And work on identifying the different ingredients and their purposes."

Zsiga spoke next. "Stealth," he said. "I can basically hide in plain sight, blend into shadows, escape detection. I would imagine the next step for me would be invisibility, if I advance any further."

"There is no reason why you shouldn't be able to advance further. Our teachers were always geared towards continual advancement of skills during our lifetimes. You may be surprised at what you could be able to do," Aslo said returning from the combat team with Iskander beside him to switch places with Zsiga.

"Your talent?" Malarchy asked.

"Seems a little strange for a big guy like me, but..." Iskander closed his fist and opened it again. There inside was a small ball of light. "I call it '*my little star*'. I can send it places and it shows me what it sees. It can give off a pretty good spark too for a little thing. Not to sure how I could expand it though."

"How far can you send it? How many can you make at once? Can you make it larger, more powerful? Can it go under water? In any weather? If you answer '*I don't know*' to any of those, that is what you should be working on," Malarchy said.

"Never thought of all that. I guess there are ways to make her better," the guard said smiling.

Malarchy signalled to Mike, William and Diana to come over. When they arrived. He looked at his chart, and back at them a few times then let out a sigh. "Good news...we have an enormous amount of defence. Bad news...we have hardly any offensive skills active. Those who are portal guards have a certain affinity for combat, which may help, but it's a long way to being able to mount an attack to bring our people back."

"We do have thirteen and assuming Willow pulls through, fourteen guardians. Not to mention the red head has some unique skills too," William added.

"Undeniably she does, but it's a far cry from growing fruit trees to fighting an army. I hate to have to say it, but, if she doesn't wake, without her skills we may be stuck. Guardians can't go through any portals without a keeper and she is the only one we have," Malarchy replied.

"If that is the case then a defence is what we will need in the end. For now though, I suggest we train as much combat techniques as possible. Prepare them to fight as a regular army and use their defensive skills to stay alive," Mike said and the others agreed.

While the new mentors were talking among themselves, Clairity approached Dezi. "You okay? I heard what you said, about not knowing what your gift was. It's not true you do know so why not tell them?"

"You should mind your own business," he snapped instantly feeling bad. "Sorry, I have known what I can do for a long time but I never wanted to end up a freak show for a bunch of people to make fun of."

"You won't it's different here," she answered. "They honestly want to develop our abilities so we can help in combat. It's elemental isn't it?"

"Yeah, fire and water, I can create both," he said looking at the ground and kicking the grass.

"You need to tell them you know."

"I will in my own time...maybe. I won't perform tricks though."

The group leaders returned to their stations to begin setting up training routines everyone could practice daily. Malarchy headed towards the sleeping quarters to find his daughter in hopes of training her with a few illusion abilities that might one day help her escape if the need arose.

At the end of the day, Dezi asked William and Mike for a minute of time alone and explained his situation, how the council made people with his abilities dress up and entertain. They were sympathetic as to why the boy wasn't willing to share his skill set with others, especially Malarchy, but also happy to hear they now had a little more offence to work with. They assured him they would train him how to use his skills in combat, not for the circus and after trying to explain what a circus was for a while without success, they gave up and let him know they were a team working together towards one goal.

Mike and William were the last two remaining in the practice field that evening, practising their combat skills against one another as they often did to relieve stress.

"Do you think any of this is going to help? They aren't exactly militia material," William said lunging forward with a sword at his friend's chest.

"They need a lot of work," Mike blocked the attack. "And you sound out of breath old man," he laughed.

"Old I am compared to you. Ten thousand of your years pass my people by for just one of our cycles. I age much slower physically than you," he replied attacking again.

"Willow too huh."

William stopped the fight and looked at his friend. The two had become close since they met years ago. "What's this about? You got a thing for the girl?" he smiled.

Mike laughed as he returned the weapon he had been using to a rack. "It's more a red hair thing. So few of us around we have to stick together."

Chapter Twenty-Four

Willow opened and closed her eyes a few times trying to focus on her surroundings. Everything was blurry. '*I must actually be waking up*,' she thought to herself.

'Y*es, we are.*'

She recognized the voice, not one of the voices she had grown up with, but one from her dream. It was Shelby.

Things were coming clearer now. There was a woman walking back and forth checking numbers on some machines which were making odd noises and writing them down. Attached to one arm was a band of material which started getting bigger. Willow winced as it squeezed the upper part of her arm so tight she though it was going explode.

"You're awake!" the lady said rushing over.

Willow was preoccupied by the wires and tubes that were attached to her. "What is all this? Ow! I want it off, get it off of me," she tried to scream, but the words came out coarse and her throat ached. Panic set in, everything was confusing her. She wanted to get up but the woman was holding her down and yelling for someone named Richard. Who were these people? Where was she? Where were Aslo and Kiera, or the kittens. She hadn't even had time to learn their names yet. What if she never did? What if she had been captured and this was all for torture? Why couldn't she speak properly?

She was fighting as hard as she could, kicking and scratching, when the man arrived and held her tightly down.

"Relax, don't try to speak. Willow, you need to relax now, you will hurt yourself," he said to her in a calm voice.

She wasn't about to relax when these people had her hooked up to who knows what. "Let me go!" She tried to scream. Again it was nothing more than a squeak and pain shot through her throat.

Richard looked at the woman and asked for something, Willow hadn't heard of before, she left for a moment and came back with a strange looking tube filled with liquid and what looked like one of Martha's sewing needles on top. She pushed on the bottom and some liquid sprayed out the top. The sight of it made her more nervous.

"Calm down now, you are going to hurt yourself. It's okay we are trying to help you," he said.

'*Help me?*' she thought, putting wires into her body didn't seem much like help. The woman moved up to a tube which had a sack of clear liquid on one end and was attached to her arm on the other. She inserted the needle and within seconds everything was flashing before her eyes. She couldn't struggle anymore. Her eyes lids closed.

"I think we need to have someone she knows here until she wakes up again. We will need William as well," Richard said sending his wife to find the others.

Mike was the first to notice Mary the nurse running across the field towards where they were practising combat moves. He left the training group and ran over to meet her half way curious as to what news could be so important she would track them down.

"Mary, is everything okay?"

"The girl, she woke up," she said while trying to catch her breath. "She completely freaked out. We had to sedate her before she hurt herself. Richard wants someone she knows and trusts in the room with her at all times till she wakes up again and he wants to see William too, as soon as possible. Maybe you could take a break here, just for a few hours, the sedative should wear off fairly quickly."

"Sure, I will fill in William and the others and we will be right over. I am sure Aslo and Kiera will want to be there as well," he said turning to head back to the others, many of whom where already staring and wondering what was going on.

Mike approached William and the two guardians first, taking them aside to fill them in. He didn't think everyone needed to know Willow had awoken afraid of the technology around her. He could see now why she would and couldn't believe none of them had the foresight to anticipate her reaction. Her world never had any doctors, medical rooms or hospitals. This would all be foreign to her and then adding on top she didn't recognize anyone she knew...It was a scenario for disaster.

After telling them what had happened, Aslo and Kiera decided to go straight over so as not to take any chance their keeper would wake up alone again. William sent everyone back to the command centre to wait except Clairity and Ashlyn. They were Willow's best friends and he wanted one of them always by her side. They could take shifts three or four hours at a time for the rest of the day. Both girls agreed, Clairity said she would take the first shift, heading over with William, while Mike and Ashlyn discussed what to tell everyone else back in the main cabin.

When they opened the door to the medical building, they saw that the guardians had changed back into their house cat forms and were on the bed beside Willow, while Richard and Mary were standing on either side. Richard had been talking to them when he noticed there was someone else in the room.

"Oh good, William, I want you to help make the choice. The IV and equipment really spooked the girl. We could unhook her from everything now and it might be easier next time she wakes. Downside is we couldn't monitor her vitals anymore and if she doesn't wake as we expect we would have to put it all back," the doctor said.

"Aslo, you know her better than me. What do you think?" William asked.

"I believe we should remove everything. She is doing well. The avian guardian looks well. I see no reason to keep her hooked up to your machines and scare her further."

"Think there is a prophecy for this?" William said rubbing the back of his neck and pacing a little "Okay, let's take her off of it all. We will give her twelve hours to wake. That should be long enough and still not dehydrate her body too much. Any longer and we will need the IV back in."

"Agreed," Richard said.

William pulled Clairity aside before leaving and asked her to keep him informed if anything happened. When she turned back, the nurse had pulled a curtain around the bed her friend was lying in, to detach all the wires in private. She was glad. The machines always made her nervous when she visited the room. She couldn't imagine all the things that were attached to Willow could feel very comfortable. Oddly enough, she thought, with everything in this world being so advanced in comparison to their home, their medical department was definitely lacking.

When the curtain was pulled back again, Clairity pulled a chair over and sat by the bed. Time seemed to drag for her. There was nothing she could do but practice her visions some in between awkward conversation with Aslo and Kiera. They were doing their best to be cordial to her, but she had never actually spoken to them before. She told herself she would feel the same if she was left alone in a room with people she didn't know, but deep down she knew she felt nervous alone in the presence of the guardians knowing they were ancient beings of great power, the true protectors of everything. After what seemed like ten cycles had past, Willow began to move.

"She is waking," Clairity said.

"It could just be muscle reflexes. Let's not get too excited yet," Aslo responded.

"No, I can feel it, she is waking up," the young prophet said.

Kiera had been curled up in a circle. Upon hearing the news she lifted her head to look at Willows face, her eyes widening with anticipation. Within moments the young girl opened her eyes a little, then again a little more, trying to focus again.

When she had regained normal eye sight, she bolted into a sitting position, wishing she hadn't immediately after. Everything was spinning. She could hear voices she recognized but couldn't make out what they were saying, it was all muffled, then she fell backwards to a lying position again. She tried to speak, but her mouth was dry and the words wouldn't form. Her throat was too sore from earlier. She had never felt so terrible before, so out of control of her senses, so weak. Lying down with her eyes closed she realized that she could focus better on what was being said.

"Relax child, please, it will take some time for you to feel better. You have been asleep for several weeks. Your muscles and eyes will need to adjust to being active again," said a voice she was very accustomed to, a voice she trusted. It was Aslo and he would never do anything that would harm her.

"Willow. It's me, Clairity. The healer here said you could have some frozen water if you woke up, to wet your mouth some. He said it would help you until you could sit and drink water. If you open your mouth some I can put a little piece in."

That was good news for Willow. She parted her dry, cracked lips and her friend slipped a little piece of ice into her mouth. It felt wonderful, cold and wet. She played with it with her tongue, letting it dance across teeth and gums. When the first piece was gone she opened her mouth again and within moments she was rewarded with another small piece of ice.

"Good, she is taking some ice chips," said a voice Willow recognized. Panic set in again, it was the man who had restrained her earlier. They had done something that made her go back to sleep. She wanted to run as fast as she could, escape to a forest and climb to where she knew no one could follow, but she couldn't if she opened her eyes she would feel sick again and she definitely couldn't walk yet. If she was in a forest she wouldn't have to. The trees would send their branches to cradle her and lift her away from all her problems, protect her.

"Don't be afraid Willow," Clairity said sensing the emotions of her friend. "It's just the healer. He means you no harm."

Was this a trick? Willow wasn't sure. She could hear Clairity's voice and she trusted her best friend, but deep down she was so unsure. Everything seemed so foreign to her, especially the way she felt. She had never been sick before, never needed a healer. She was scared.

A new voice appeared. "She is frightened, this experience is overwhelming for her, she is not yet able to communicate verbally. Earlier her screams were pure adrenaline. Now she is calmer. It could take awhile. I suggest only voices she knows well talk in her hearing range until she has use of the rest of her senses."

"Shelby?" Kiera said. "Is that you?"

"Kiera, my friend, yes your keeper spared my life, without her I would still be broken beyond repair."

"Lasel?...and your keeper?"

"Prisoners, deep beneath a castle at the heart of a stone mountain, in world ruled by madmen convinced they deserve retribution. I am afraid they are lost to us, with many more," Shelby said.

"I am sorry. Is there nothing we can do?" Kiera replied.

"Perhaps, but now is not the time. Willow must recover fully before we discuss the possibilities. Unfortunately, I believe that may take weeks if not longer. She was subjected to a taste of the torture I endured, that broke me. We must tread carefully, make sure she is back to normal before she takes on any more."

Willow wanted to shout out to them she was fine, but the dryness of her mouth and throat still only let her make a few squeaks. Truth was she wasn't fine, she was dizzy, felt sick to her stomach, very tired, and weak. She had never felt like this before and she didn't like it.

"Perhaps I can help steady her senses," Aslo said as he joined with her becoming a picture on her arm in the same spot where Shelby had previously been.

"How does that help?" the doctor asked.

"When the Leander...feline guardians become one with another being we give some of our traits to that being. In Willow's case, when she is joined with Aslo or myself...or one of our children, she receives the benefit of agility, stability, additional balance and night vision to name a few," Kiera said.

Willow felt more like herself almost instantly and her mind began to race through information of what had happened over the past weeks to share with Aslo.

'Shhhhhhh child, now is time to relax. We can discuss everything when you are better. I don't want you to strain right now,' Aslo's familiar voice sounded in her head.

'Okay, but I feel better with you here. Do you think I could open my eyes without spinning in circles now? I should very much like to go to the restroom and then wash up some,' she replied back so that only her guardian could hear.

'Yes, slowly open your eyes and adjust, then try to sit up first. No sudden movements everything you do must be slow. Also keep in mind you haven't used your muscles for a bit and they are considerably weaker now than you remember.'

She followed Aslo's advice opening her eyes slowly and adjusting to directly in front of her first, then slowly looking around to see everyone. She made sure she was in control of her eyesight before attempting to slowly move to a sitting position. Once she sat up, Clairity offered her a cup with some water, which she took a sip from. After a few sips she found she could speak, just a word or two and the feeling wasn't pleasant, but it was progress.

"Thank you," she mumbled to her friend for the water. Shortly after she asked if she could try to get up with one word, *'restroom'*. Clairity agreed to help her if Richard would allow it. She let out a little sigh of relief when the healer agreed to let her try walking.

As soon as she set her feet down on the floor she realized what Aslo had meant. Her knees were buckling at first not used to supporting her weight. Clairity supported her so she didn't fall flat on her face. After a couple steps, she felt a little more steady, but couldn't imagine she would be running across tree tops anytime soon.

Clairity helped her wash up and dry off. It wasn't until she looked in a mirror that she realized what she was wearing. It was an off white colour and like an apron of some sort. To her shock she had nothing on underneath and the back was open except for the part that tied together at the neck. Someone could see her backside if she was walking.

"Where are my clothes," she screamed as loud as her voice would let her.

"It's okay, just relax," her friend answered. "They had to take them off you to keep you clean and washed while you were out."

Okay? She thought no part of this was okay by any means. What part of people seeing her without clothing would ever be okay? She spent her lifetime making sure she was covered as much as possible.

"I am not leaving this room without clothes," Willow said in tears.

The sound of rain outside was clue enough for Kiera that something was wrong with her girl and she headed into the restroom to see what was wrong.

"She wants her clothes," Clairity said.

"Of course, I will find someone to bring her some. There was an extra set of her keeper clothes in the backpack you brought through the portal," Kiera

211

answered and headed off to find someone to bring the outfit over to the medical centre.

She returned quickly with Mike carrying the backpack containing clothes. Clairity came out to retrieve the bag and quickly returned. Willow was still weak her friend didn't want to leave her for long even resting in a chair. After dressing she tied her hair back off her face. It was limp and dull and even seemed somehow thinner than she remembered. She made a comment about how horribly thin she looked in the mirror. Her face was pale and her bone structure was peaking through as if her skin was transparent.

"I look sick," she said.

"You have lost weight and muscle. There is a medical program in this world they call physical therapy, which people need to use to rebuild strength after being in a bed immobile as long as you did. It could help you. Aslo and I have discussed it with the medical healers and think it is the fastest way for you to recover, although it will be a long time," Kiera said.

"Time is something we don't have a lot of. There is an invasion coming and it will come here, we just don't know how long we have to prepare or try to stop it," Willow said leaning hard on her friend.

"Don't worry," Clairity said. "Nathan found a prophecy about the bird guardian. It says when you wake up things will be better."

"What prophecy? What did it say?" She hadn't had time to review all the prophecies yet and Nathan last time she saw him hadn't read the book yet. She was happy to her that someone was working on figuring out what they all meant.

"Nathan shared the book with me," Clairity said just before reciting the prophecy exactly as it appeared in the book.

' A race forgotten shall appear again, in need of intervention

one soul so pure shall see the cause and alter what could be,

devastation averted, a world now saved,

one life shall be the reward, within its mind a soul has been lost

and another shall fall to slumber, the signs on doors to show the way,

with rest and time life shall renew and mind shall mend

all shall emerge with questions answered

life preserved and new hope granted.'

"See it fits perfectly," her friend said in an excited voice.

"I am afraid I am too tired to think right now, but keep in mind prophecies can have messages for more than one person. There is usually more to them than just the obvious, or else they would be...well...useless," Willow replied.

"I see what you mean," Clairity replied with a puzzled look on her face. "So how do we learn what they mean?"

"I think the best we can do is all know them, study them and figure out a rough time line. Then when the time comes, hopefully we will see the answer and use it to our advantage." Willow was showing signs of stress from all the activity.

"We best get you back into bed now," Kiera said and Willow agreed. She was tired and sore.

Back in the main room of the medical centre there were a few more people now and she was definitely glad she had clothes on so no one was staring at her bare backside. Mike and William were speaking to the healer man, while looking at her walk slowly across the room with concern. Shelby was sitting on a chair and Ashlyn was doing something at the table beside where her bed was. As she came closer to the bed she saw there was a vase of water with something in it. A flower she thought, straining her eyes to see that far. No, not a flower but a branch.

"Ashlyn, is that..." Willow's knees buckled and she collapsed, luckily on the bed so she didn't hurt anything else.

"Willow!" her dream walker friend screamed.

Everyone rushed over to her side and helped her into the bed again. She closed her eyes for a few moments before finishing her question "Is that what I think it is?"

"I thought it meant something in the dream when it fell so I brought part with us through the portal. I was hoping it would make you feel better."

Willow interrupted her. "Ashlyn you are brilliant, you know that? I need to get outside," she said trying to stand.

"You are too weak to go anywhere little girl," Mike said.

"If this means what I think it means, it is the most important thing that could happen to any of us. Carry me if you have to but I need to get to the middle of the field by the sleeping quarters."

"The training fields? What for?" William asked.

"Just please trust me. I am getting tired very fast I need to do this now," Willow answered grabbing the branch from the vase. Aslo appeared back in his cat form beside her on the bed.

"Do you really think this will work?" the guardian asked.

"I think so, as long as I have enough energy..."

Aslo nodded to Mike to go ahead and move her as requested.

"Okay squirt hang on tight," Mike said picking her up and heading out the door to the training yard.

There were still groups practising combat skills outside and word spread quickly that something strange was happening. Soon every building emptied and everyone was watching Mike carrying her. At first she couldn't help but feel self conscious. She looked like a fragment of the strong girl everyone had known, thin and sickly, not even able to walk across a field, but then she realized her task was far more important. If she was right, this could turn the tides for them. It was all there in the prophecy Clairity had recited. So obvious, this had to be what it meant.

Chapter Twenty-Five

Without the guardians connected to her she was much more wobbly on her feet. She noticed the difference as soon as Mike put her down.

"I will have to sit to do this," she said to him.

"Sit to do what? Are you going to tell me what you think you are going to try to do?" Mike asked.

"Just help me get down on the ground...please. I would prefer to do it with some dignity rather than a face plant." she laughed a little, which made Mike smile.

"Alright," he said helping her down on the ground.

"Thank you. Now back up and keep everyone a good distance away. It is important no one gets too close," she said. All in all, she figured for a normal human man he was a great addition to their team, even if he could be a bit of a jerk sometimes. In fact, there were several men and women who were a gift to have on their side.

After everyone was a safe distance away, she mustered up her strength and drove the branch into the ground. She took a deep breath and lifted her arms up. A gold sparkle appeared around the branch like a small twister surrounding it, getting larger and larger until it looked like it touched the sky.

"She is failing I can feel it," Clairity yelled out.

Mike and William went to move towards her, but Aslo changed to his full form and blocked their way.

"She has to do this. I will not let you interfere. This is the most important thing she will ever do. This is what she was destined for. If she fails all will be for nothing," Aslo said snarling, his large teeth showing.

Moments later Willow fell over. Her body lying motionless on the ground. The twister dissipated and revealed a large tree with sweeping branches. No one moved, was Willow okay? Was it safe to move closer to see? William ran his hands through his hair and let out a large breath of air he had been holding through the whole display.

"Can we help her now?" he asked.

"Wait, just a few more moments," Aslo answered.

"She could be dying. We could help her," Mike yelled.

Sobs were coming from the crowd of people now as they watched Willow's body lying limp and lifeless in a pile at the base of a tree. Everyone feared the worst.

Although there was no breeze in the air, the long sweeping branches of the tree began to move. They picked up Willow's motionless body and lifted her high, surrounded her with a glowing aura. Physically her body began transforming back to the girl she had been before she helping the avian guardian. Her hair broke free from the tie that bound it and swayed gently around her face, brilliant red, thick and radiant, perfectly complimenting the return of the light bronze colour of her skin. The transformation mesmerized everyone watching. Willow sat up and opened her eyes, their colour spectacular. The sprinkling of red against a sea of green and blue portrayed an image of dancing flames on water. She looked around, reaching out to touch one of the wispy branches of Acacia the ancient tree of justice. It astounded her. She had believed at one time, Acacia to be a story made up to entertain children. Now she realized everything she had known before was a lie. Eventually she would have to relearn the truths of her world and uncover all the secrets that had been hidden from her and everyone else.

"You have saved me from an eternity of torture, always burning in necrid flames but never able to extinguish my life. That part of me has now withered since you called me here through that branch. I owe you my gratitude," Acacia said breaking her train of thoughts.

"I had some help with that, they are a good team. We could use your help," Willow said.

"I am bound by the same rules as the guardians. Sworn only to pass judgement on the worst crimes, committed by those who choose to act on that part of themselves capable of committing the most terrible acts possible and enforce punishment if needed. I cannot intervene directly in your search or daily physical battles. These things you must do for yourselves. I can help you in another way, provide tools to help you help yourselves and when the time comes, you will know and call me."

Everyone had been so preoccupied by the grandeur of the great tree that no one had noticed a girl had approached the base of it. Willow looked down and saw Jade, well what looked like it could be Jade. She was somehow different, her hair was without style, lacking brilliant colour, her face and eyes had lost their luster. She was almost homely compared to her former self.

"I am here for your decision, my punishment for the atrocities that I caused," Jade said bowing her head down.

"Hummm, yes it is true you did make some poor choices. Are you sorry?" Acacia asked.

"Yes, of course, but that doesn't make things better," Jade cried.

"No, it doesn't, but you can make things better than they are now. What has happened has happened, hopefully you learnt from it."

"I did," she sobbed.

"Then return to your father. He needs you now. When you go forward from today help others to see and change. Your part in our future is not yet over," Acacia said and paused for a moment before adding, "Whether within an individual or an entire kingdom, there is the ability to do good, bad or nothing at all. The choice is ours to make and to choose one way does not mean we will always choose the same again. Remember what you feel now and make the most of your choices in the future."

Jade did as Acacia said and returned to her father who had been nervously watching from a distance. A look of instant relief came over Malarchy's face as he saw his daughter walking back. A display of any form of affection had never been his style but he too was somehow different and he hugged her tight as if he never wanted to let go.

A bright glow filled the sky with shimmering lights of purple, red, green and gold. A dusting of sparkles of gold and silver rained down on William's property and the people outside watching the events of the evening unfold, disappearing on touch. The branches of the great tree set Willow down on the ground safely. She noticed immediately she felt strong and healthy again. She was herself.

"Thank you," she said.

"It is you that I thank. You will find now and over time you have what you need to continue. I am anywhere you need me if you ask," Acacia replied.

Willow started walking towards her friends, she noticed a glow was circling around, Shelby was flying above and found a branch to land on. Aslo and his family nodded at her and joined the avian guardian at the tree.

When she came closer to her friends she saw something unusual. They had all changed. Even without them moving, she could see they were stronger, faster, more powerful and there was something else. Willow stopped and smiled. She looked down at the inside of her arm and there it was, the symbol, she was a portal guard and so were many of the others. She walked over to each and turned their arms to see, Clairity, Ashlyn, Jessie, Dezi, Pete, Neil, Camile, the younger Victoria and Nathan, even Jade and Malarchy all had the portal guard symbol. To her surprise others had it as well, new additions to her family, Mike, Sarah, Richard, Mary and others who had aided William over the years had been given the honour and with it extended life and perhaps other gifts, only time would tell.

Shelby left her perch and circled around in the air. It must feel good to be free again Willow thought, watching her soar high above then dive down and land on Ashlyn's shoulder and disappearing. Could it be? She ran over to her friend and asked to see the shoulder where the bird had just been. There was a picture of a black bird looking happy and content with her new home.

"You're a keeper!" Willow said.

"Me?" Ashlyn said in disbelief "Why me? How?"

'I knew in the dream we were compatible, that you would be the one to carry me forward until I find my keeper and mate again. There will be other guardians who have lost their keepers and will need you. I can help you develop your gifts in dreams if you let me,' Shelby's voice said to Ashlyn alone.

She looked at Willow with excitement, "I can hear her in my head. Is that what it's like for you too? All this time you never told us."

"Voices in my head wasn't something I wanted to share, especially since I didn't know where they were coming from until recently," Willow replied.

Looking down she noticed two of Aslo and Kiera's children were rubbing against her legs and purring. It had a pattern to it, a rhythm. She could hear a message in it, like a song almost. They were telling her they loved her. They needed to help another, but they could reunite again later. They would always be a part of her. She smiled knowing there was another new keeper to be born tonight and she thought she knew who.

The two cats left Willow and walked over to her friend Clairity, rubbing against her bare ankles a few times before appearing as pictures on her lower legs.

The three girls hugged they had something new to share now. Willow realized how much she had missed their together time in the forest, now they had a reason to go off on their own and discuss keeper matters.

Looking up she caught a glance of Diana walking away. She hadn't been chosen to join the ranks of guards. It wasn't because she wasn't worthy Willow thought, no Diana Waddington had always been an outstanding person. Like a light bulb clicking on inside her head, she understood. It was because Diana was Lance's aunt. She was the one King Cornelius was looking for, that their enemies considered imprisoned somewhere, stolen from them.

Chapter Twenty-Six

Willow, was already joined with Aslo and Kiera when she caught up with Diana entering the main cabin. The command centre was empty. All of its usual inhabitants were still outside buzzing with excitement. Mike and William walked in behind her before she had a chance to say a word. The look on the storyteller's face was solemn. It was clear she didn't understand why she had not been chosen to join the ranks of portal guards and felt it was some shortcoming of her own doing. Nothing could be farther from the truth. The guardians agreed with her.

"Don't be upset," Willow said, unsure how to start the conversation. How do you tell someone their brother is an evil maniac bent on the destruction of everything.

"What's wrong?" William asked.

"I wasn't chosen," Diana said. "I am not as worthy as all of you. Perhaps I do not belong here."

"There must be some mistake," Mike said.

"No, I don't think so," Willow replied turning her attention to Diana, "But, it isn't what you think."

"Then why?"

"To protect you," she answered. "Your brother, his name is Cornelius, a king?"

Diana nodded with a look of curiosity in her eyes. "How did you know that?"

"In my dreams I met his son, your nephew...they are the ones who attacked us and they are searching for you."

"What?" the storyteller said letting out a gasp. "Why?"

"I was hoping you could provide some details to fill in the blanks of what I know," Willow said.

Mike and William looked at each other then back.

"I have a feeling there is a story here we need to hear," William said.

"It begins somewhere in the time of the blood wars," Willow started. "That part of the story I have little detail about, but something happened and according to them it was the three races, snakes, spiders and sea creatures, that remained guardians, and the cats, wolves and birds that split from them. In other words, they believe we are the bad guys. Skip forward to the time of the portals and the splitting of worlds becomes an evil plot to control all creatures and enforce our vision of what the world should be...It's all very backwards, but very real to them. In this version of reality, you were...stolen from them, against your will. In fact they believe all those chosen were taken as hostages to stop possible uprisings."

"That's insane!" William said.

"Insane or not, they truly believe they are righting a wrong. That they are justified in their actions and saving worlds from us. They mean to destroy every guard and keeper."

"I chose this life," Diana said, tears falling down her face.

"I know, but when the time comes, when you meet your brother face to face, I believe it is important you do not show the mark of the portal guard. Can you tell us what you remember?"

Diana sighed. "I was young...a teen of your age. It was the end of the blood wars. Our kingdom had managed to stay clear of the conflict, but it came close to our lands and one day my parents, the King and Queen, were out visiting a border town. They were killed...No one invaded us. It was a spill off of a fight from the neighbouring kingdom...not planned. They were simply in the wrong place at the wrong place. It is possible we would have been a target next."

"My brother took his rightful spot as King the next day. He was full of grief and anger. I begged him not to act on emotion, but he ordered that his guards obtain magical blood and drink it in case an invasion occurred...only as a precaution. He never intended to use it as a weapon. I tried so hard to change his mind. We had been so close to each other. He wasn't a bad person." She paused for a moment and wept.

"Against my advice he and others drank the blood...It was never necessary. The portals were created almost immediately after, but the damage was done. When the guardians came and asked me to go with them, I agreed. My brother offered to help as well, but he was denied. I believe it was because he slayed those creatures and drank their blood. It had tainted him...he was no longer pure and innocent. He was angry, so very angry. They didn't want him, a king...I left, but I was given extended life. This was a very, very long time ago. How is he still alive?"

"The serpents must have felt his anger. They gave him venom to drink. It runs through the veins of all his family giving them gifts, including extended life. In exchange he raises armies, seeks out other worlds, destroys or imprisons our kind and if he finds them he will release the other ancients from the worlds they are now contained in. They plan to remove the barriers between worlds and rule all in the end. Nowhere is safe," Willow said.

"Well, now we know who the enemy is and why, just the where left to figure out," William said breaking a few minutes of silence. "Anything either of you two remember and want to add would be helpful. The prophecy deciphering team will need to know these details. Maybe something in that book will lead us in the right direction." He placed his hand on Diana's shoulder. "There is nothing you could have done. Many men went mad after drinking the blood, power hungry, believing they were better than others. Once he tasted it, his fate was sealed. Willow is right. There may come a time when you will be face to face with him again and you have a better chance of survival without the mark."

"I do not wish to survive and live a lie. I am one of you!" she yelled.

"It's not just you. There may be others whose fate rests in your hands at the time. There is a reason for everything. You must trust Acacia has one," Willow said.

Diana looked at her surprised. She obviously had never considered there could me more at stake than her own life. It made more sense now. There were possibilities for what her role in the future might be. She nodded indicating she understood and took a seat quietly reflecting on everything that had been said this evening.

"Nathan," she said after a few minutes. "Can we tell him first before the others? It is his family we are talking about after all."

"Of course," William said. "I am asking him to come here now." Having a telepathic link to almost everyone would definitely have its advantages. It would also mean a lot more people talking about things he didn't necessarily need or want to hear and at all hours. He would have to have a lesson or two on when it is appropriate to use the link.

"Gran!" Nathan said moments later running in. "Isn't it great! Did you see? They called me and without saying anything. Not even leaving the room. Think I can call them when I find something or when I need help or if I want a cookie."

"No!" Mike said sternly causing the boy to turn and look at him.

"I think there are some things you need to do for yourself still. Imagine if you were working hard and heard twenty people all ask for soap in the shower or a drink outside. It would ruin your line of thought," Diana said.

"Soooo...no cookie?" he asked scrunching up his nose.

"No, cookie," Mike said smiling this time.

"We will have a class or two to go over what is appropriate to ask and not, as well as to teach you all how to communicate with just one person at a time rather than all of us," William added.

"Phew," the boy said motioning as if he was wiping sweat from his brow. "I was worried there I might always be in trouble."

Diana laughed.

William had already turned his attention to Willow. She wasn't moving and was staring at the picture on her arm. The picture was fading in and out.

"Surely that doesn't mean that you are being reconsidered as a guard," he said. The others turned their attention to the red head as well now.

Willow looked up and the two black cats appeared. She wasn't sure what it meant, but Aslo would answer for her.

"No...Willow has a unique talent. She must have developed it during all those years we were together. She was a child and no matter how much we drilled into her no one was to see the pictures on her skin, a slip up most certainly should have occurred. We always thought it was dumb luck, but now it appears she can hide marks on her skin on command. We never noticed because we were the pictures. No one else did because they never knew we were there."

"The picture hiding doesn't mean it's gone?" Mike asked.

"No, it still there and still has the same effect as it does on anyone else, just it's invisible and she can choose to show it again when she wants to. A talent that may come in handy for her one day," Aslo responded.

"I don't suppose you are tired?" Mike said smiling at Willow.

"No, definitely not. I think I have had more than enough sleep for today," Willow answered.

"How about I show you some sights of this world? Promise you'll love it," he said.

The invitation caught Willow off guard. She hadn't ever expected Mike to be nice to her. Things really had changed while she was sleeping. "Sure, I would like that," she answered. It was the truth she was excited to finally see some of what she had read in books and it still bothered her she didn't know exactly where she was.

"Make sure you two are back for the meeting tomorrow morning," William said smiling. "Oh and Mike, you might want to remember you still don't know how to keep all your thoughts private yet."

Chapter Twenty-Seven

Mike went to get a vehicle and a few minutes later pulled round in what he called a Jeep. It had no top or doors, but other than it looked pretty much like a small truck. She hopped in and Mike leaned over and pulled a belt from the side of her seat around.

"It's for safety," he said, connecting it to a metal-piece by the edge of her seat.

For the first time, she noticed he had a musky smell to him, manly and strong. She liked it and when he sat back in his seat, she had an urge to lean towards him, close her eyes and let the aroma fill her senses.

Probably not a good idea she thought blushing, then hoping no one else heard her thoughts, causing her to blush a little more. She also realized she was grateful Aslo and Kiera decided to stay behind and help Clairity and Ashlyn adjust, last thing she wanted was for anyone to think she had gone boy crazy.

"Everything alright?" he asked noticing the flush colour on her skin.

"Yeah great, I was...just thinking how odd it is having to worry about what everyone else hears. I mean, am I safe having thoughts to myself? I am used to guardians hearing everything but not everyone."

"I know what you mean, but I don't think they can hear everything. It has a trigger, emotions I think control it. William can request the mental connection with other guards on and off. May take us some time to get used to it all," he answered with a big smile on his face.

The drive itself was fairly uneventful. No top on the jeep meant a lot of wind making hearing someone talk difficult. She found she had to yell for him to hear her at all and even then she wasn't sure he actually heard everything she said. He would nod and agree mostly, probably trying to be nice. She quickly decided not to speak till they stopped, settling on taking in the surroundings instead. They past fields and farms, animals and forests. Occasionally, they drove through a town, with lights and store fronts with signs that captured her imagination. This was all so much more in every way than she had been used to and nothing she had read even began to describe what she was seeing.

When they finally stopped, they were on top of a hill of some sort. Looking down she could see a city below all lit up. It was spectacular. There must have been thousands of lights, everything was so bright. She imagined that if she was down there it wouldn't even look like night at all. In the distance she could see a body of water. She hadn't yet gotten used to big areas of water, especially ones that were deeper than her height. The thought terrified her. Nathan had read a few books on boats and swimming, but it wasn't something she felt the need to experience anytime soon. Past the water there were more lights, another town she thought, there must be many in this world.

"How many towns are there?" she asked.

Mike laughed. "To many to count," he replied.

"Really? I mean I had an idea it was big from the maps but this goes way past anything I could ever imagine. How do you keep track?"

"We don't really," he answered. "Generally people live in one area. They get to know their area of the world pretty good, but if they go outside that area, they use a map or if they go long distances they hire someone to show them around."

"Can we go down there? See what a town that big looks like up close?" Willow asked.

"Sure, hop back in. If you are hungry we could stop for some food somewhere. I am sure we could find something open," he answered.

"I thought we passed all the farms on the way here. You mean there is land to grow things down there too?" she asked.

"No, it's complicated to explain in full, but food is sent to places where they prepare it and serve it to other people for money," he said.

"Money?" That word was not something she had learnt about in any book yet.

Mike let out a big breath of air, "I can see this isn't going to be easy." He couldn't help but smile at her, she was staring at him with such interest. "In your world everyone had a job, correct?"

"Yes," she answered.

"Here it's the same. Because there are so many people, we assign values to jobs they do and a system to exchange services. You do a job, you get money for it, then you use the money to get things from other people."

"I don't have any money," she said with a frown.

"I do. I will get you something," he promised.

He started driving again. She was confused by it all. Everything was so big and there were so many people, so many things. As they approached the town, there were more and more vehicles on the road and people out walking about, even at night. Some had strings attached to animals, she made a mental note to ask someone about that later. She had been right, the lights made everything bright. They stopped at a building.

"This is a fast food restaurant," he said. "They can make your food in a few minutes. What do you like to eat?"

"Apples, berries, tomatoes, oh and I very much like peaches," she answered.

"They have burgers and fries that are pretty good," he said.

"What are burgers and fries?"

"Hamburgers, ground beef cooked and served on a bun?" he said trying to explain.

"Ground beef?" she asked

"Meat, from a cow," Mike answered.

"How do you get it from the cow?" she asked with a look of worry on her face.

Mike must have missed her concern. "Well it is dead first."

"Dead?" she screeched. "You eat dead creatures?"

"Yessss..." he said unsure if that was the right answer.

"Oh I would like to go back now I think. I am sorry. I was taught the only thing worse than eating something that has died is killing it to eat." Thinking of the blood wars she added, "Or drinking its blood."

"Okay. Well, I didn't realize you were a vegetarian. They do have salads, fries are fried potatoes. There are other options."

"Vegetarian? I maybe should have read a few more books before experiencing your world in person," she answered.

"A vegetarian is someone who doesn't eat meat, just vegetables, fruits, some eat cheeses and drink milk as well, breads and grains," he said.

"Yes, I guess that is what I am...I can grow what I need anywhere," she said, looking around. "You go ahead and have whatever it is you like to eat."

"How about we go somewhere else. There is something I want to show you. This I think you will like."

Willow agreed and before long they were walking across a field of cars towards bright lights and loud sounds. There were people everywhere, all ages, some holding hands, some using weapons that squirted water, some with gigantic stuffed creatures. People were laughing and screaming and a few vomiting. There was loud music and all different things that spun around in circles. In the middle was a gigantic wheel that caught her attention.

"It's a ferris wheel...a ride. People go on it for entertainment," Mike said. "Do you want to go on it?"

"Yes please," she answered smiling.

They waited in a line for quite a bit of time, however Willow hardly noticed. She was too busy watching the big wheel turn around, carrying so many people and their faces going on and off the ride. Then it was their turn. She could hardly control her excitement. The attendant showed them to their seats and listed off some rules about not standing or leaning over while the ride was operational. Then he moved on to the next couple. The wheel turned to let another group off and on. She sat watching all the people and attractions on the ground. She could see everything. Mike pointed out a few interesting places they could go to while they were there. The wheel went round a few times. The feeling was indescribable. Willow couldn't imagine there was much better to experience anywhere in this world than that ride. All too soon it was stopping and letting people off and the two of them were back on the ground again.

Mike took her hand, leading her over to a stand selling all different kinds of foods. He bought her something he called cotton candy. It was pink and sweet and melted in her mouth like she had never felt before. Then they were on to another ride, which spun round in circles and made her scream, not so much a frightened scream, but an excited one. Everything happened so fast there. They played games. He won her a fake creature, which was soft and hug-able and after a few more rides, they tried apples with a candy coating on them. The taste was sweet and tart at the same time.

The two spent time looking around, just walking through the crowds of people and seeing everything. This was by far the best night of her life. She had never done anything more exciting and free. Willow felt a tug on her arm and turned to see a short older lady dressed in bright colours with scarves and jewelry. She wore dark makeup around her eyes and a bright red lipstick covered wrinkled lips.

"Be forewarned on Hallows Eve those who are not of this world shall take to the streets, blood shall flow and death shall follow. Your presence attracts what we cannot explain. Your destiny is written. You best make sure you listen," she said in a voice with an unusual accent.

"Hey!" Mike said turning around and realizing someone had a grip on Willow. The woman turned and disappeared into the crown.

Willow felt everything spinning. She had felt this far too much since coming to this world. Her knees buckled and everything went black. Mike reached her just in time to catch her head from hitting the ground.

Chapter Twenty-Eight

When Willow woke in the jeep, they were already turning the corner to enter William's property. Looking at Mike she could see the concern on his face. A waive of guilt came over her for ruining the evening. She had been nothing but a pain all night, especially with the eating meat thing, which had caught her off guard. She was sure that could have been handled better and then passing out in the middle of what Mike had called a park. Why did the woman's words affect her so much? Or maybe it was a combination of the excitement of the evening, everything all together had just overwhelmed her. She did know one thing. She had been having the best time of her life and she doubted he would want to take her anywhere new again.

Mike parked and came round to her side. He hadn't realized she had woken up, but even seeing her eyes open, he lifted her out of the seat and carried her towards the main building. She didn't mind, not that she was tired or light headed but she enjoyed resting her head against his shoulder and inhaling his aroma again. It made her feel safe and warm, something she couldn't remember feeling, at least this strong, before.

William, Aslo and Kiera were still in the command centre. They had sent everyone else to get a good night's sleep, except a few men who were doing perimeter watches. Mike put Willow down on the couch and the others hurried over to find out what happened. He retold the story as far as he knew it, leaving out the part about freaking over eating meat, which Willow was quite happy about. Then it was her turn to fill in about the woman. She described the old lady and her clothes, jewelry, makeup and voice, then she told them what she said.

'Be forewarned on Hallows Eve

those who are not of this world shall take to the streets,

blood shall flow and death shall follow.

Your presence attracts what we cannot explain.

Your destiny is written. You best make sure you listen.'

"A prophecy?" Mike asked looking at William.

"I don't know, but I think we should treat it as one. Tomorrow everyone is back to the prophecies. If something is coming we need as much information as we can find," he answered. "As for you young lady, perhaps some time in bed just to make sure you are really okay?"

"No...no, I am fine. I think it was just too much to process at once, the lights, the people, the noise. It caught me off guard. I can help," she answered. "You need me. I have a way with the prophecies."

"She is correct. We do need her insight, since it seems so many of the prophecies are about her in some way," Aslo said. "It makes sense she can decipher them. I also think we need a training session on this world before anyone else ventures into populated areas."

"Agreed," Mike said making Willow feel horrible. She wanted to tell him she had fun. She hadn't even had a chance to thank him for taking her yet, but she couldn't, not in front of others, it would be too weird.

"Okay off to bed with you," Kiera said. "They are short handed tonight, everyone is resting for a big day tomorrow so Aslo and I are helping patrol. We will see you in the morning."

"Are you okay to walk?" Mike asked.

She wanted to say no. She wanted him to lift her up and carry her to her bed, and place her down gently, but answered '*yes*' with a meek smile instead. The whole walk to her sleeping quarters she was beating herself up inside for giving up her opportunity to thank him for taking her, for showing her so many things, to let him know she had the best night of her life and to apologize for being rude about the food. She figured he would probably never talk to her again.

She hopped back in bed and the kittens immediately joined with her. She made a mental note she still didn't know their names yet and needed to learn them. She could hear little giggles in her mind, which made her smile. Even with all the sleep she had lately, it didn't take long until she drifted off into a deep slumber. There was no fear of night scares tonight. She would dream of one thing, being back at the park having fun with Mike.

"Willow...Willow!"

She opened her eyes and stretched before realizing Clairity was standing over her. "Hey," she said still trying to wake up.

"We have a meeting, remember?"

"Is it late?" Willow asked, worried she was sleeping way too much.

"No, but we will be late if you don't get up and get ready," Clairity said handing her friend some clothes to change into.

Willow did as requested. She got up and did her morning routine of washing, brushing and changing. Stopping to look in the mirror she realized for the first time, she didn't hate what she saw. She thought for a moment Acacia maybe had pity on her and changed her a little.

"Do I look different to you?" she asked Clairity without taking her eyes away from the mirror.

"No, why should you? Did something happen?"

"No, maybe it's the light, it's nothing," she answered.

The kittens remained in bed for the day. All the voices could be confusing for them as well, so it was the best choice and Aslo had already spoken to them about it. After seeing them settled, all curled up together in little balls of fur, the two girls headed out to the training field to meet the others.

They were the last to arrive. Mike was working with Jessie, Dezi and Pete already, and didn't even look up to acknowledge her, but William did.

"Nice of you to join us ladies," he said. "I guess we can begin then. Right, everyone gather round. In this first exercise I want each of you to close your eyes and imagine a line connecting yourself to a person who is here, someone close. When you have that concentrate on saying '*hi*'."

Willow chose Clairity and said her '*hi*'. For a moment she thought everyone had chosen to say hi to her. Voices were coming at her from all directions, all mixed together. It hurt.

"Let's try one at a time," William said still shaking his head from the noise.

It didn't seem to matter who he chose. The '*hi*' rang out to everyone. It was Willow's turn. She said '*hi*' to Clairity again and looked back to William.

"Are you done?" he asked. "Who did you speak to?"

"Clairity," she answered.

"I heard it. Did anyone else?" her friend asked.

No one else did. *'Score one for the good guys,'* she thought. Clairity and Ashlyn also had the technique down. They figured it had something to do with being keepers and the natural telepathic link that gave them. The three of them were excused to practice among themselves with bigger messages.

The training went on for several hours and then broke for lunch. Willow decided as soon as everyone returned she would take Mike aside and thank him for last night. She went back to the training site early to find him, but Mike didn't return.

William went over a list of rules for when to use the telepathic link and when not to, using Nathan's cookie story as an example, which made Nathan happy and most everyone giggle.

He ended the meeting asking everyone to practice and report any unusual abilities that may arise, warning that for some, advanced fighting skills could mean the ability to call weapons to appear. The skill had only been seen in proficient fighters before. He didn't think any of them had to worry about it yet, but at the same time didn't want a limb to be lost during practice fights, or worse.

Willow had been having a hard time concentrating, she was wondering where Mike had gone. Why had he not returned with the others from lunch? She had the urge to run up and ask William right there in front of everyone, but thought that might seem a little strange. He had been nice to her but they certainly weren't a couple. It was more likely she was reading something into the situation that wasn't there. He had made her feel warm and safe. It was nice. Her mind turned to Lance, he was the opposite. He gave her feelings of excitement and danger, made her feel wild and alive. She hadn't thought of the prince at all since just after the dream, but now she could see his piercing blue eyes locked on hers, feel the way he watched her. It was a different connection and yet the same.

"Willow!" William yelled, breaking her trance.

"Sorry," she replied. Looking around she could see that almost everyone had left and she was standing there looking silly. "I was thinking about...the prophecies," she added figuring it was the most believable thing she could say.

"How about thinking about them with everyone else inside the command centre and maybe...I don't know...sharing your thoughts?" he said.

"Yeah sure," she answered. The tone of his voice had told her this wasn't the time to ask about Mike.

Nathan was sitting at the table with Diana when she walked in. The first order of business was for Nathan to share the book with her, so she would remember every prophecy. The group had already implemented a policy of sharing '*The Portal Prophecies*' every week to ensure it remained fresh in their minds. They also worked out of the book itself.

"So where should we begin?" William asked as Sarah took a seat beside him. Kiera and Aslo were already sitting on the table waiting for everyone to settle.

This was her chance she thought. "Aren't we going to wait for Mike?" she asked. She couldn't seem to think of anything else.

"No, he had something personal to take care of," William said.

"When will he be back?" Nathan asked.

Willow covered her mouth as she sighed in relief. She was glad the boy had been the one to continue the conversation, as much as she wanted the answers, she also didn't want anyone knowing she might have developed a crush on Mike.

"Not sure. We should concentrate on the prophecies," he answered.

> *'On the outside flesh rots, but under is fine*
>
> *the captors look dead, the prisoner fine,*

no one notices, no one hears, a scream for help disappears

hidden in darkness, unable to move

the ones with power have something to prove

look for the signs that something is near

unusual and strange, that people fear

under a store which sells that which can be made

you will know the place by the woman with the blade

some powers real, some not

rope, fire and water punished the lot'

Willow wasn't sure why she had chosen to read this prophecy out loud but she felt the need. She had no idea what it meant either. Maybe her mind wasn't clear enough to do this today. All her thoughts went back to boys over and over.

"Okay, so any ideas?...Willow?" William asked.

"I don't know. It popped into my head. I just had a feeling it was relevant. It mentions signs. I think since Ashlyn's interpretation helped her find me, she took signs to mean symbols of something. We should use that as a start," Willow answered. "We are looking for something unusual and strange that people fear. Didn't you say people of this world make things up for whatever they can't explain?"

"Yes," William said deep in thought. "It could be the signs we are looking for are something the human world created to signify something they fear. I guess we should start some research into myths and legends." He walked into a back room and came back with a pile of books. "Start with these Nathan and share them. I will start on the computer."

Weeks of study went by and the group found out very little about the prophecy. They looked at various different stories about monsters and strange happenings. A few Willow tagged as requiring further attention at a later date, including The Black Mountain in Australia, The Bermuda Triangle, The Lost City of Atlantis and creature sightings such as Yeti, Bigfoot, Lockness Monster and mermaids. But some how none of them seemed to fit the situation.

Nathan found reference to one type of creature thought to have rotting flesh called a zombie, but after reading hundreds of books and watching hours of shows on the creatures, no one could find any signs as to where you would locate them. It seemed this may be the one being that did not actually come from another world and was just from someone's imagination. Not knowing for sure, they continued research. Anxiety levels were rising. They were going no where with this prophecy. William finally suggested they move on to another and Willow reluctantly agreed. She had a feeling deep inside this was important, but other prophecies were probably just as important as well.

The group decided to look at the prophecy from the amusement park for the rest of the afternoon. They started with Halloween delving only slightly into the history. The in depth analysis of the celebration was something William would gather books and information on, for them to look at tomorrow.

They learnt from Sarah, that Halloween night had become a holiday when people would dress up in costumes which resembled monsters and celebrate with candy and feasts. The most common scary costumes being vampires, ghosts, mummies and witches. She explained as she went along what each was supposed to look like.

Diana remembered the story about Sarah's family. "Perhaps that each of these creatures, like the vampires, could be from another world and just named differently," she said.

It made sense and fit in with the prophecy so William agreed to find as many books as possible on each of the creatures so they could be studied separately. Feeling like they had at least accomplished something, he dismissed the group till the morning.

There was still no word from Mike. William didn't seemed concerned, but there was talk around camp that he had left them, or run off with some girl. Something was wrong and Willow knew a way to find out how. She just needed to figure out how to suggest it without looking as if she was some stupid girl with a crush, stalking him.

Ashlyn and Clairity found her at the edge of the tree line. The three girls decided to take a well deserved afternoon alone to catch up and gossip, all guardians left behind. When they were safely hidden away in a tree fort Willow had created, Clairity spoke.

"I actually had another reason for wanting us to talk alone. I have a feeling...something is wrong. I know William and the others don't trust my intuition much, but you two, you know I am accurate," she said. "It's about Mike."

"About Mike?" Ashlyn spun around, her eyes sparkling with interest. "Everyone is wondering what happened do you know?"

Willow was amazed they were saying everything she had been wanting to say, asking the same questions she had wanted to ask.

"No, I don't know exactly, but it isn't good. I think he is hurt," Clairity responded. "My visions are getting stronger but none of it makes any sense. People dressed in black robes so you can't see their faces and big black pots over a fire, chants of something I don't understand."

"You wouldn't happen to know where would you?" Willow asked.

"No, I don't know enough about this world to recognize anything."

"We should tell William," Ashlyn suggested.

"No, I don't think he would believe us," Willow said leaning back on a branch so her head hung upside down. "No, if we are going to help him we need to figure this out ourselves." She paused for a moment to sit up, before adding, "What if you bring us into your dream and we search for him? If we can find him and talk to him or see more about where he is at least then we would have something to go to the others with."

The two other girls agreed to try that evening.

Chapter Twenty-Nine

The three girls met up after everyone had gone to sleep. It hadn't been hard to convince the guardians to take patrol overnight again. Years of being constantly joined with another being meant Aslo, Kiera and their family enjoyed having some freedom and Shelby was glad to stretch her wings and soar like she never thought she would again. Each of them took their place on a bed with Ashlyn in the middle, ready to fall asleep and hunt for clues. They moved the beds close enough to each other so that they could hold hands falling asleep, hoping the bond would help them meet in the dream world. At the very least it couldn't hurt. All three swallowed a sleeping pill to make sure they went in at the same time. It hadn't taken much to convince Richard the noises from their new telepathic connection were keeping them up and they needed help to fall asleep.

Ashlyn was the first to open her eyes. She was in a familiar white room, which she had decided to call a staging room. It was where she started every dream now. There were doorways that led to other people or dreams she could enter. She began looking for the symbols and calling to her two friends. She heard a knocking noise and followed it to a door, which she opened to find Willow. The two then continued searching doors together until they came across one that was a mirror. The two girls looked at each other and decided to try the handle. Clairity was waiting on the other side. They were together now, but that was the easy part.

It felt like they were walking in circles for a very long time calling out to Mike, but without answer, when a different door appeared. It was all black with gold carvings on it that none of the girls had seen before.

"I think that's it," Willow said.

"Feels like," Clairity agreed.

"How did I know you were going to say that. We couldn't pick a door with daisies or sweets? Noooo. We have to pick a door of darkness and unknown." Ashlyn shivered. "Go on then. You two open it."

After exchanging glances, Willow grabbed the handle and pulled the door open to take a peak in. The three girls didn't even have to step through. They were already sucked into the middle of this dream.

It was a town of some sort and it was night time. Although there were street lights, they were flickering on and off so they actually gave off very little light. Willow imagined how the Leander's night vision might have come in handy about now, but shrugged it off as lesson learned, pride gets in the way of practicality. That led to questions of whether Ashlyn could bring all of the guardians into a dream as well. She shook her head. These were questions for another day.

The girls slowly started walking down the street trying to take in as much of their surroundings as possible and look for clues or signs as to why they were there or where they were. They were definitely walking down a road. It was smooth and even. There were store fronts and businesses, all appearing to be closed. One boasted a sale on magic wands, while another had ingredients for '*All Your Potion Needs*' written in the window. There were also people, all wearing dark brown or black. Hoods of cloaks covered their faces, although they all turned to face the three girls as they passed by. Willow realized how badly they stood out, wearing bright white, even if it was a dream.

The next block had six stores. Three on each side. At least they assumed them to be stores. There were no windows to see in and the doors were closed.

Each one had a sign that hung above the door with a different picture on each. On one side of the road was a black cat, a raven and a wolf. On the other was a spider. The second was a sea creature, which Willow identified as a kraken, having seen pictures of it in a book earlier that morning. The last was a snake.

"Where did all the people go?" Clairity asked knowing neither of her two friends had an answer.

Continuing on to the next block it was exactly the same stores, with the same signs, and again and again. Willow grew a small flower in her hand and placed it on the ground in the middle of the road. Then the three continued walking until they came to the same flower at the same place Willow had left it behind them.

"Guess that means we need to pick a door," Willow said.

"Why do I have a feeling you aren't picking the fluffy kitty door," Ashlyn said.

"Serpent?" Clairity asked.

"Serpent," Willow agreed heading over to the wooden door. Without waiting she pulled it open and stepped through.

The girls were greeted with a blast of musty sickly sweet smelling air. The store was dimly lit with candles. Willow could make out some dead flowers and plants hanging from the ceiling, a few of which she recognized as ingredients Micca had needed to make a potion to help the Shinning boys. There were some dead animals, stuffed to make them look alive. Everything was dusty and old. Books lined the walls, some for making spells and potions and others for meanings of herbs and scents. For a moment, she thought she had seen a copy of *The Portal Prophecies'*, but how could that be? She took a step closer but stopped when she heard a voice.

"I'd be careful not to touch anything my dears," sounded from behind them. Willow swung around, she recognized the voice, there in front of her was the woman from the park, still dressed the same and holding a large knife. She went back to cutting up something black and slimy that looked like it might have been still alive.

"Where are we?" Ashlyn asked.

"Did you not find what you were looking for? There is a button there for help." The old woman pointed to Ashlyn's side.

"That wasn't there before." She reached forward with one finger.

Before Clairity and Willow could scream 'NO!', the young dream walker reached forward and pressed the big red button marked help and a trap door in the floor gave way sending all three crashing to a lower level.

"Brilliant!" Willow said.

"How was I supposed to know that would happen," Ashlyn answered.

"I don't know. Maybe when she said don't touch anything it might have been a hint," Clairity barked. "I know it was for me."

"Oh," she answered. "I thought she meant anything else."

"Could you two get off me now?" Clairity was patiently waiting squished beneath the weight of both of the other girls.

The three stood up and dusted off, for a dream they still felt the aches from the fall. If they thought it was dark upstairs, it was a hundred times worse downstairs. None of them could see a thing.

"Ashlyn, you can control the dream world, try to create some light," Willow said.

"I'll try but I haven't been very successful in the past," she replied, concentrating as hard as she could on light.

Willow felt something in her hand. She looked down and then said "Matches? Really? Couldn't be a lantern, ball of light, torch, one of those flashlight things Mike uses?"

"Told you I wasn't very good at it yet."

"Never mind, maybe we can find something to make a torch out of. Feel around." Willow crouched down to the ground and felt the dirt covered floor for anything that could help.

Clairity found a piece of wood and after trying a few matches to light it, the girls decided that wasn't going to work. They definitely needed something to light to get the wood burning, but there wasn't anything.

"Wait," Clairity said. "I have an idea!" She ripped her white dress and wrapped some of the material tightly around one end of the wood.

"Brilliant!" Ashlyn yelled.

Willow used a match to light the cloth. If nothing else, it would give them a chance to look for something better or move on to another hopefully better lit room.

The hallway they were in was made from grey bricks. The whole area was damp and had a musty smell to it which was less than pleasant.

"Kinda glad we didn't pick spiders right now," Ashlyn said imagining the cobwebs and creepy crawlers all over a basement behind that door.

The hallway seemed to go on for a long stretch, then ended at a choice. They could go left or right. Both ways were equally dark. There were no signs to tell them where to go.

"So now what?" Ashlyn asked.

Willow examined the walls, looking for any indication of where they were heading, but couldn't find anything. "Guess it's up to you Clairity, choose."

"Me? Why me?" Clairity asked stunned.

"Kinda thought you were the psychic. Go with your gut," Willow answered.

"Gut...gut...Okay. We go left because nothing we choose can ever be right in this place," she replied.

"Okay, left it is. I like that reasoning."

"I don't," Ashlyn mumbled following behind the other two.

They came across several empty rooms before they heard what sounded like mad dogs barking in the background. A few seconds later they found themselves in a room filled with smaller rooms that had bars on them, like cages. People were reaching their hands through the bars grabbing at them, some moaning for help, some screaming in pain. They couldn't see their faces.

"Do you think Mike is one of them?" Ashlyn was on her tip toes trying to see to the back of the cages.

"No, everything tells me he isn't in there," Clairity answered.

Willow had the same feeling. He was there somewhere but not with these people, somewhere else. Up ahead on the other side of the room was an old fashioned wood doorway. She headed towards it and swung it open.

Sitting upright in bed, Willow opened her eyes, the prophecy they had been working on so hard, it was about Mike. He needed help.

GLOSSARY

These terms may be found throughout The Portal Prophecies. Not all terms may appear in every volume. Additional terms may be added to future volumes as needed.

Acacia – An ancient tree with consciousness, thought to be one of the first creatures in existence. Its appearance is depicted as a type of willow tree.

Achaear – An ancient spider race. Once guardians, the Achaear preferred a life dedicated to their own race rather than the protection of others.

Albino Assassin – A race of beings white in appearance with deadly black wings which power their shadow and teleportation magics. Their knowledge of combat exceeds that of all other known races.

Allaren – Avian Guardian who takes the form of a black bird to bond with another being.

Ancients - Those in existence before mass population of the worlds. Thought to be some of the oldest living beings. There are different aged Ancients, ranging from supreme beings to guardians.

Apopp - One of the most prominent Xiuhcoatle (Serpent Race). He controls all contact from his race with the main world.

Aquanor - An ancient sea creature race. Once guardians, the Aquanor preferred a life dedicated to their own race rather than the protection of others.

Blood Wars – Wars created by men in order to expand their kingdoms. The blood wars were started by certain ancient races to gain advantage over guardians. Men became obsessed with obtaining and drinking the blood of magical creatures to gain temporary abilities that aided them in battle. The wars ended in the creation of the portals.

Council - A group of mentors. Originally appointed to train new abilities in those who were aiding the guardians. After a prophecy was made about the end of the guardian home world, the power of the council was taken over by men and was quickly corrupted.

Coven - A group of witches who practice magic together. There are usually thirteen members.

Cycle – 1 cycle is 10,000 years in main world time.

Displaced - The essence of a living being which was removed from its body before physical death occurred.

Dream Walker – An individual with the power to enter and control dreams. They can also call people into their own dreams.

Empowered, The – The underground newspaper for Empyral and the magical.

Empyral – Beings living in the main world, but having come from other worlds. They are generally happy to take residence in the main world and do not pose a threat to society.

Faeries – A magical humanoid sized race. Their eyes are a shimmering white and silver. The females have wings. Not much is known about actual Faeries.

They rarely interact with other races and it is much more common to find one of their many cousin races.

Frostica – Ice faeries. Their bodies appear humanoid, but their faces are more animal like. They are about two feet tall. Their bite is deadly.

Glaquool – An advanced bodiless race, made up of different gases, who crave experience and knowledge. They discovered they could hide in objects, which on touch allowed them to displace the essence of the being and take its place.

Green-eyed Recluse Collegiate – A school specializing in illusion magic.

Guardians – Combination of ancient races who protect the rights of all beings to exist and grow in which ever direction they choose. If faced with a choice, they will always chose to protect the greater good.

Gypsy - Term used to describe a group of witches who travel around constantly, hiding from a powerful necromancer.

Hannulate – Peaceful and fun loving creatures who live in magical realms. A direct cousin to faeries. They were once one of the most beautiful races to exist. During the blood wars they were forced to adapt to survive, by developing sharp teeth and razor claws that could extend at will.

Keeper- individuals who can host guardians to allow them to pass through portals. It was believed a keeper could only carry two guardians of the same race at a time.

Kriller - a race of the most intelligent creatures to live. The speed at which their brain works causes changes in the formation of their facial features They communicate to each other telepathically and then work together to complete necessary tasks.

Leander – Feline Guardians who take the form of a black cat to bond with another being.

Light - a person able to read energies and can lend energy to another person to enhance their natural abilities.

Main World – The modern day world. It is the largest realm and connects all of the worlds by portals.

Medium - A witch who specializes in contacting the deceased.

Necrid Flames – a blue flame that engulfs and destroys all living material.

Necromancer – A witch who specializes in death magic.

Olcsanka -A wolf/bear guardian who takes the form of a wolf to bond with another being.

Portal – Doorway to another world that can only be opened by guardians. Once open any creature can use it if it remains active. Guardians can only pass through a portal when bonded to a keeper.

Portal Guard – Those chosen to protect, who travel through portals and ensure the safety of all realms.

Portal Prophecies, The – A book of prophecies made by Iris and Raven prior to the wars and recorded by Diana. There is also a book written by a gypsy named Estonia by the same name.

Portal Stones - The four corner stones required to open any portal.

Samhain - The witches' new year, when the divide between the realms is thinnest, allowing supernatural activity or contact.

Sleeping-Sands – The most prestigious of the schools for the empyral.

Terra former – A person with a rare ability to manipulate weather and soil to sustain life. They can also grow plant life on command. There are few documented people with this ability. The extent of their abilities is not known.

Terunji - People living in the main world who are completely oblivious to the magic around them.

Transmutton – Yeti.

Underground, The – A hidden city. It's inhabitants are all magical, whether from the main world or other realms.

Vamprite - A race of shape shifters led by a young prince, Drake. During the blood wars they learnt that drinking human blood could keep their people young, strong, and beautiful. The main world knows them as vampires.

Wand - A wooden rod used to channel any form of magic and turn it into any form of physical magic the user needs.

Whisps - Bodiless beings who keep their form generally in the shape of a sphere composed of raw energy, or light. Considered a possible explanation for ghosts.

Winks - The smallest of the Faery family. A scale for them would be from the size of a fruit fly to that of a house fly. They all have wings and, unfortunately, a mischievous nature. Although they mean no harm, their pranks and jokes often lead to destruction. Considered a possible explanation for poltergeists.

Witches - A name given to any humanoid with unusual amounts of magical powers. There is some difference between main world witches and those from other worlds. There are different types of witches, practising different types of magic.

Wizard – A witch who practice alchemy and potions. They have a more scientific approach to magic. Wizards can still channel magic through a wand.

Xiuhcoatle – An ancient serpent race, once guardians.

Yeti – Abominable Snowmen.